# RESCUED BY DADDY

SERENITY STABLES
BOOK 3

CASSIE HARGROVE

*Dante, AKA @whisperdevil666, thank you for guiding me on how to make Dameon as realistic as I could for Abigail.*

## CONTENT DISCLOSURE

Thank you so much for coming to read Rescued by Daddy!

I just wanted to give you a heads up that this book DOES deal with abuse from a parent as well as on page cutting/self-harm and fighting the urge.

Please proceed with caution if these subjects are hard for you to read.

- Cassie

# CHAPTER 1
## ABIGAIL

As kids, adults will tell you life is unfair. What they're neglecting to mention is how badly it will fuck you up the ass, and most times, you have to just lie there and take it. You feel a loss of control over things happening to you because you don't see a way out, or maybe there isn't one.

The latter always been the case for me, anyway, but not for much longer. In a couple of weeks, I will finally have control over my life, and I intend to take it. Even if it means living on the streets.

As long as I'm away from *him*, I don't care where I end up.

Stopping in front of the store, I turn to the window and freeze. "Shit!" I hiss, looking around to make sure no one is nearby.

I can't have anyone see this. I'm always careful to cover the bruises up so no one finds out. I'm not even sure how I missed it before leaving the house this morning.

Was anyone walking by me close enough to see this? Dad will kill me if anyone finds out what he does to me behind closed doors. The mayor of Haven Hills can't be seen as an abusive prick, after all.

When I don't see anyone nearby, I look around at the surrounding vehicles. One of the Serenity Stables trucks is parked down the street, so I bolt toward it, hoping and praying they're as trusting as everyone believes they are. I need the doors to be unlocked. If they're not, I'm going to be late for school at this rate.

Trying the door, I curse when it doesn't open and start to turn away when it beeps. Glancing through the windows of the truck, I see Dameon Easton heading this way, and curse under my breath. Of course, the person driving the truck just had to be one of the owners.

God, my luck sucks. Dameon Easton is tall, sexy, and he gets on my nerves like no one else on the goddamn planet. Today, he has his dark blonde hair styled in a way that makes him look a little dangerous and it sends shivers down my spine. I can't see his green eyes from here, but I can envision them with ease and I bet they're filled with annoyance.

He always seems like he's annoyed with the entire world unless he's with his family. Even then, his sister is probably the only one he truly smiles for.

Seeing how Dameon is preoccupied with his phone, I decide to risk it. I cannot go to school with this bruise showing without garnering too many questions that I can't, and don't want to answer.

I open the door, searching the cab before my eyes land on a thick sweater lying on the passenger seat, and make a quick grab for it. Quickly pulling it over my head, I start moving out of the truck just as he looks up from his phone. He's less than ten feet away now. His clenched jaw is all I need to see to know exactly how annoyed he is at my presence.

I smile, hopping out of the truck and slamming the door.

"Abigail," he growls, noticing his sweater. It smells like him and it's distracting the fuck out of me, but I just smirk.

"D," I respond, backing away slowly before turning and running.

"Abigail Davies, get your ass back here!" he hollers, but I can tell he's not coming after me. He should know better than to think I would listen.

"Fuck you, D!" I shout back, continuing to run until I'm far enough away I know he won't bother chasing me.

It's not that I enjoy stealing or pissing Dameon off. But I need this sweater. If I have to choose between stealing or someone seeing the bruises, I'll choose theft every time.

No one would ever believe that my father is capable of the abuse he doles out. Even if they did, he'd make me pay for it, so I need to cover my tracks.

*Just a few more weeks.*

"Time to get to school, Abby," I whisper to myself, readjusting the sweater to make sure it's pulled down comfortably as I make my way there.

"Hey, baby," Ted whispers into my ear at lunch, and wraps his arms around me from behind.

I hold back the sigh of annoyance and lean into him. "Hey."

I put up with him because he's a decent lay. He

has the ability to get me out of my head for a while when I desperately need it, and that's a huge bonus. But deep down, I know he wants more than I'm willing to give.

"Meet up later?" he asks, kissing my neck. I'd love to meet up with him for a quick fuck, but I'm not sure it's the best idea right now.

"I have to get home. Dad gets off work early tonight," I tell him, moving out of his arms so I'm not distracted. It's a lie. He'll probably get home extremely late and drunk as hell, but I need that alone time.

"I can come over," he states, trailing off when I give him a look.

He knows better than to suggest that, considering I don't let anyone near my house. He just wants to get his dick wet, and I'm not exactly in the mood. Just the thought of someone seeing the way Dad behaves makes me sick to my stomach.

"Sorry." He holds his hands up, backing away from me a little. "Text me if you change your mind about meeting up later," he says, giving me a hurtful smile before walking away.

"When are you going to tell the poor guy you aren't dating?" my best friend Rose asks from behind me.

Rose Carver has been my best friend since we were little, and I love her to the ends of the earth and back. People always used to comment about us looking like twins, but I never understood it.

Sure, we have the same lean body type, we both have shades of light blonde hair and blue eyes, but we aren't the same. Rose isn't hardened on the inside from years of abuse. She still holds this peaceful grace about her that I lost when mom died in the accident that should have taken me too.

It's been years since I held that hope and positive outlook on life that she still possesses. So, no, we don't look alike. People don't really say that anymore now, though. Not since she kept dressing in feminine clothing and I chose a more punk rock, emo wardrobe. But she will always be my bestie.

"He knows," I tell her. "He's just in denial, and I can't help him with that."

"You're a killer, babe. It's totally harsh, and I love it." She cackles.

"I just don't feel the need to commit to one person when I'm out of here in a few weeks," I remind her, and she sighs.

"I'm really going to miss you. You know that, right?" she asks, and I give her a sad smile.

"You could come with me." I wish she would, but

I know she can't. She would never leave her family behind, and I understand that. I just don't have the same grievances. There is absolutely nothing keeping me here in Haven Hills.

"I can't, and you know it. I just know I'll miss you." She closes her locker, looking at me with sad eyes. "I can't believe you're just three exams away from graduating months ahead of everyone else."

I smirk, thinking about the conversations I had with the guidance office last year. I told them I needed to make this happen, no matter what. That I would either graduate by the time I turned eighteen, or I'd drop out. They didn't like that, so they worked with my teachers to come up with a plan.

Haven Hills isn't like a lot of other towns and schools. The teachers here really care about what happens with us once we leave here. I've heard it's not the same everywhere, so I'm grateful for that small blessing. At least I'll be set up for college in the fall.

After I find a job and save up, that is.

"I've been working my ass off, Rose. I need to get out of here," I say, and she nods.

"I know, babe, I just hate it."

She does know. Parts of it, at least. She knows that Dad is a drunk and can get mean from time to time, but she doesn't know the extent of the damage that he can inflict. I've always been able to cover up or explain away the bruises in a way that no one has ever been suspicious... I think.

"Hey, we'll keep in touch. I promise," I tell her, pulling her into a hug.

It's a promise I know I can keep.

## CHAPTER 2
## DAMEON

"You're pissed because she stole your sweater?"
Joe asks me as he tosses another bale of hay onto the
pile.

He's one of two older brothers, and always trying
to get inside my head. Clearly, today is no exception.
He's taken on the role of peacemaker between the
three of us and our little sister. Especially after Lana
was hurt by her bastard ex.

When we discovered that being around any form
of anger could be extremely triggering for her, we
worked out how to make sure we limited the possibility of that happening.

That's why I'm out here in the barn, stacking
bales of hay while my brother psychoanalyzes me.
I'm having a hard time shaking my frustration with

Abigail for how brazen she was, and I need to work it off before going into the main house. I think part of my irritation is from not knowing why she drives me mad when no one else does.

"Sort of," I admit, heaving another bale onto the pile. I'm actually more frustrated that she gave me the good-ol' fuck you, followed by her nickname for me. She's the only one that calls me D.

"Sort of?" he questions, stopping to stare at me. "What does that even mean, Dameon?"

I sigh, stopping to wipe the sweat off my brow with my forearm. "I can't explain it."

I can't. The way Abigail has always gotten under my skin is something I can't put into words. She's almost ten years younger than me, so it's not like we have the same friends or circles. But there's something about her take no prisoners' attitude that calls to me.

She's always been brave and snarky, and I admired that about her when she was a kid. As the daughter of our long-running mayor, it's ballsy to say the least. But now that she's not a child anymore, it makes me want to spank the shit out of her for being a brat—in a completely non-creepy way.

I swear to fuck, Abigail Davies needs a handler.

*Yeah, Dameon, good thought. Now you're thinking*

*about being said handler and it's completely wrong. Even if her long blonde hair and bright blue eyes are like a siren call, tempting men into the depths of hell.*

Jesus, I need to get ahold of myself.

Maybe I need to find a submissive to play with at the club that has her fire. It would give me the chance to burn off some of this energy, and brats are always fun.

"Do you like her?" he asks after tossing another bale of hay.

"No!" I say, shaking my head. "She's seventeen, man." I grunt, continuing to work.

"Almost eighteen, if I remember correctly," he says innocently enough, but I stop and narrow my eyes at him.

"Do you like her?" I question, feeling myself get a bit heated.

I don't necessarily like her. I can't. She's too young for me. Abigail is too innocent to really comprehend my sadistic desires. I need a submissive that loves pain and begs for it in order to feel satisfied as a Dom. It's the main reason why I have a membership at *Ignition*, the BDSM club a ways out of town.

Not that the club has been doing anything for me the past few months. Each time I go I end up supervising rather than participating because nothing is calling to me anymore. I'm beginning to think there's something wrong with me.

Shaking my head to collect my thoughts, I narrow my eyes at Joe. Him being interested in Abby? Hell no, I don't like it.

"If I did?" he taunts me, trying to get me worked up.

"You're too old for her," I tell him matter-of-fact, and he nods.

"I'm aware." He shrugs. "Just playing Devil's advocate."

He likes to do that. He and Carl both do. Out of everyone in our family, I'm by far the most hot-headed, so they like to play the 'what-if' card so I can see things from a different perspective.

Having two older brothers can be a pain in the ass, but sometimes I swear these fuckers test me on purpose. Assholes. Quickly smiling to myself, I throw the last bale onto the pile and turn back to Joe with a straight face.

"I'm thirty-two years old. I'm not about to go after an eighteen-year-old," he states firmly. He's acting like I've somehow offended him, and I scoff.

"I'm twenty-seven. You think that's any different?" I ask, not sure what to make of his thought process on this.

Joe stops what he's doing to give me an incredulous look. "Trent is twenty years older than Lana. Your nine on Abigail is nothing."

Shit, he has me there. I know our little sister is really happy with her man, and he's really good to her. But me and Abigail? It's not even in the same realm of similar. Trent is nothing like me, and I don't see any similarities between Abigail and Lana either.

"There's more to it than age, and you know that," I remind him, and he nods.

"You're right, there is. I'm just trying to get you to see if there's a particular reason she gets under your skin. That's all, man," he says, pulling his gloves off.

"I don't know, Joe. I can't tell you why the girl frustrates me so goddamn much. If I figure it out, I'll let you know."

He smirks, shaking his head. "Yeah, you do that." Then walks off laughing.

Fuck, older brothers are a pain in the ass.

I'm following him into the house when I'm instantly met with some form of torturous Hell. Jesus fuck, this can't be happening again.

"Hey, firecracker," I greet Lana, thinking I'll get the friendly and loving response I always do.

"Yeah. Hey," she says, staring at the television and waving her hand, not even looking my way.

Shaking my head, I move into the kitchen where Trent is sitting with Joe and Carl.

"What type of alternate-reality hell is happening in that damn living room right now?" I ask, glaring at Trent.

The look he gives me right says he isn't happy with my attitude, and it's enough to settle me a bit. The bastard is huge and scary, not to mention completely in love with my little sister. Usually, his anger wouldn't intimidate me, but he seems extra on edge today and it's mildly terrifying.

"Watch how you speak about her, Dameon. I won't hesitate to shoot your ass if you use that tone toward her again," he threatens, and I swallow.

He's completely serious and I fucking know it. Whatever is going on with Lana has him on edge, meaning we all need to take note and keep an eye out for her.

In my defence, I was already in a rough mood before being met with the that musical shit in the living room. I've never enjoyed musicals on a good fucking day, and Lana watching *Teen Beach Movie* just blasted me back to her teen years.

"Sorry," I sigh, holding my hands up. "But why is

she watching a Disney musical? Isn't she too little for that?" I question, looking between him and my brothers.

Trent is my sister's fiancé, but also her daddy and dominant. Not that I like thinking about that aspect of their relationship, but being a little has helped my sister recover from the trauma her asshole ex put her through.

*Stop thinking about it. He's already dead, and this line of thinking is just going to piss you off more.*

As far as their dynamic goes, to each their own. I may not be a daddy per-say, but I've been around Lana enough to understand how to care for her. I'd be there for any little that needed help and guidance as long as it was temporary and platonic. I wasn't made to be a daddy like Carl and Trent.

Trent sighs. "She has exams, and she's making herself sick with stress. She was struggling to let everything go and be little, then decided she wanted to try being in middle space for a change," he explains, shrugging, and I nod.

Her choosing to trying being a middle actually makes a lot of sense. I'm not going to pretend to know what happens in their dynamic, but I do know my sister and how worked up she gets worrying all the time.

She's never been one to just let it go when she needs to study, so I can see how being more teenage-like could be beneficial to her right now.

"Does she need to see Evans?" Carl asks before I get the chance, and Joe snorts.

"She's not dying, guys. She's stressing over her tests. She's always been like this. We just have to ride it out and remind her to eat, drink, and sleep. Once the tests are over, she'll be back to our sweet little sister instead of a teenage demon."

"I don't like it," I tell them, Carl and Trent nodding in agreement.

"Things have changed since she was actually a teenager. I've got her, I promise. She gets this one movie, then it's back to studying. After dinner, she's not allowed to do anything but relax, and I will make sure she does," he says with a smirk, and I'm out.

Carl gives a nod of approval while Joe chuckles, but something sad crosses his face, making me pause before I can leave.

All four of us guys have always known we were dominant. Joe, though? With his bipolar disorder, there have been times where he's needed to be cared for. We're fairly certain he's a switch with submissive tendencies, but the dominant side takes over more times than not. But he doesn't like to talk about the times where he's been submissive—maybe even little—and we know better than to push him.

I share a quick look with Trent and Carl, seeing that they've noticed it as well. Good. That means we can all watch out for him in case he spirals. I pray he won't, though. He usually hates himself afterward, which makes the healing process even harder on him.

Who knows? Maybe he'll call Derek—Travis' psychiatrist brother—and talk it through this time. It's the first time Joe has had the option to talk to a professional who truly cares at the same time he's going through an episode, so he might take advantage of that.

# CHAPTER 3
## ABIGAIL

I CAN'T BELIEVE I FORGOT TODAY WAS THE anniversary of Mom's death. I've been living alone with my father for fourteen years now, enduring the alcoholism and abuse he continuously throws my way.

Sometimes I try to remember if he was ever like this before she dies, but I can't recall him even raising his voice. Not until he lost Mom. That's when he changed, but it's hard to remember a time before all of this darkness and anger. The hatred brewing inside of me is just too strong now.

Grabbing the bottle of perfume I keep hidden behind my mattress, I stop to grab my little package from the nightstand before sitting on the floor. My bed is the best place to prop myself against for things like this.

When I open the little square of silk, it reveals my blissful escape. Sharp edges that give me freedom from the pain threatening to swallow me whole. It's the only thing that stops me from lashing back at Dad when he comes home, using me as his personal punching bag.

Laying the blade back down, I quickly roll the sleeves of D's sweater up, unable to fathom taking it off right now. It's as though it's giving me some form of comfort. Maybe it's because I'm swimming in it, so it feels like a giant hug or a weighted blanket. I wish it was enough, but it's not. I'm still struggling to breathe through the pain.

Picking the blade back up, I don't waste time before sinking it into my skin, sighing in relief when the blood rushes to the surface. Watching blood flow from the fresh cut produces a release of serotonin as I imagine my emotions escaping me in a physical form.

It's the only form of escape there is for me.

It's that or sex, and I already hurt Ted today. I cannot deal with his emotions on top of my own right now.

I make a few more cuts and watch as the blood

slowly stops flowing. Once it has, I reach into my pocket for the paper towel I'd prepared for this moment. After cleaning them up, I roll the sleeves back down and check the time. I can never spray Mom's perfume unless I know Dad won't be home for a while, and tonight being the anniversary of her death, he won't be home for hours.

"I wish you were here, Mom," I say into the room after spritzing her perfume into the air.

Vanilla. It's the only calming scent I like.

I've barely gotten the bottle and blade back to their rightful places when the front door slams. Panic takes hold of me like I've never felt before.

Fuck. He's going to smell her perfume.

"Abigail!" Dad bellows, stomping down the hallway and shoving against my door. It's locked.

"Dad! You're home early," I squeak out, barely able to push the words past my panic.

"What the fuck is that smell, Abigail? Is that your mother's perfume?" he snarls through the door.

"No. I—"

"Don't lie to me, you little bitch. Open this door before I break it down!"

I whimper in fear, standing to do as he says. If he has to bust it down, he'll just make my punishment worse. This is what I get for trying to feel close to her. It's like he doesn't want to be reminded of her existence, even when him losing her is what made him the asshole he is.

"Dad-" I cut off when his hand wraps around my throat, stealing my air.

"Why does your room smell like her?" he hisses through his teeth, the smell of alcohol already pouring off him in waves. God, he's been at it all day. Did he even go to work?

"B-bed," I rasp, unable to catch a breath.

He drops his hold on me, and I crumble to the ground, watching as he throws my mattress off the bed. He destroys everything in his wake until he finds the bottle I keep hidden away.

It's not the original bottle that he keeps locked away in his room, but it's the same brand. I wanted to have a memory of her with me when I was having a particularly hard day.

He stops throwing things, gently lifting off the cap and smelling the perfume, and or a moment, time stands still. I witness the pain he carries with him daily over her, but it's gone all too soon.

With a loud roar, he throws the bottle against the wall, and the glass breaks into tiny pieces. As the smell of vanilla envelopes the space, tears start falling from my eyes in streams matching the perfume dripping down my wall.

My one moment of weakness is my first mistake. You never take your eyes off the danger in the room. A hard slap lands across my cheek before he's lifting me by my throat again, glaring at me with untamed anger.

"It should have been you," he says to me, not for the first time. And not for the first time, I really wish it had been me.

"D—" I croak, unable to breathe as he squeezes my neck tighter.

"Shut up, Abigail. You deserve this." He pulls his fist back, and I know what's coming.

It's not the first time he's beaten me, but it will be the last. When he leaves this room tonight, I'm leaving and never coming back. Fuck waiting until I'm eighteen. I can hide from the law for a couple of weeks.

His first punch lands on my ribs, directly followed by a loud crack and excruciating pain. Fuck, that's going to be bad.

Dropping me to the mattresses tossed on the floor, he goes for his belt, and the blood freezes in my veins. There are two things he could do right now. One of them I would have never expected to happen, but I've never seen him like this before either, so who knows?

The other? Well, I've got scars on my back that tell that story already. A few more won't make a difference.

"You're nothing like your mother. She was everything perfect in this world, and she was taken from me!" he screams, ripping the belt from his pants.

I breathe again when he doesn't try to undo his pants, finding some comforting in knowing he isn't going to go there. At least he has that going for him. The pain, I can deal with. Raping me? He'd never take another breath.

He stares down at me for a moment, taking in my fear before wrapping his belt around my neck; something he's never done before.

Maybe I'll finally die and find the peace I've been longing for.

## CHAPTER 4
## DAMEON

I DON'T KNOW WHY I EVEN TRIED TO GO TO THE CLUB tonight. I insisted Joe come along with me, then stood at the bar and turned down any submissive wanting to scene with me. It's what I've been doing the last several times we've gone, but I continue to try. And fail.

Something is wrong with me.

"You didn't scene tonight," Joe says from the passenger side of the truck.

I shrug. "I think something is going on with me. Might have to talk to Derek if it continues," I state, sighing in defeat.

"You think something is wrong with you? Like what?" he questions, turning in his seat to face me as much as the belt will allow.

"If I knew, I wouldn't need Derek's help, would I?" I don't take my eyes off the road. I refuse to see the pity and worry in his eyes right now.

I get it. It's not normal for me to be so... particular. But something has been stopping me from agreeing to any and all scenes. I just don't know what. If I did, I'd tell it to fuck all the way off, because a man has needs, and I'm usually more active than most.

"Maybe you're just finally growing out of the playboy phase you've been living in since you discovered sex." He shrugs, smirking a little.

Bastard loves taunting me, but maybe he's right. Maybe I am just growing out of it. Seeing both Lana and Travis find their life-altering loves has shifted something inside of me, and for the first time, I think I might actually want to feel something outside of strictly sex and control.

"STOP!" he shouts, drawing me out of my thoughts as I slam on the brakes.

"Fuck! What is it?!" I ask, my heart racing as I look toward him, but he's already out of the cab.

My eyes turn back to the road, taking in the scene before me. I snap to attention, getting out of the truck and moving to where Joe is crouched over something. Someone.

"What is it?" I ask, halting when a battered and bruised face comes into view. "Christ," I hiss, feeling sick to my stomach.

Lying in front of me with her hair splayed out on the dark pavement, is Abigail. And I'm not sure she's breathing.

"Call an ambulance," Joe orders, but I already have my phone out.

"Here." I shove my phone at him before leaning over Abigail and gently touching her wrist, trying to find a pulse. "Hey, sweetness. Can you hear me? It's Dameon Easton."

She whimpers, coughing a little before drawing in a sharp breath. I share a look with Joe as panic recedes a little now that we know she's alive.

I'm not naïve enough to think she will stay that way if she doesn't get help, and fast. Her breathing is erratic and shaky, and she refuses to open her eyes.

"No," she whispers, her voice laced with fear and pain. "No touch," she cries.

My head shoots up to check on Joe, and he moves back to kneel beside us.

"Fifteen minutes," he states, holding the phone to his ear. "Hopefully sooner, but that's the longest it will be before the ambulance finds us."

What the fuck happened to her? Did she get hit

by a car and they ran off? What is she even doing all the way out here on her own?

Questions run rampant in my mind, but I refuse to ask any of them right now. I just need to keep her alive and conscious. Or semi-conscious, I guess.

"Abigail, can you hear me?" I ask again, and she groans. This time, she doesn't try to move her body, which clearly means she's in more pain than we know.

"They can... hear you," cough, "in Alaska, D," she groans, making Joe snort.

"So goddamn sassy," I mutter, shaking my head and moving my hand from her wrist to to weave our fingers together.

"Abigail, it's Joe. I'm here too," he says quietly, trying to ease her pain.

"Party's all here, then?" she jokes. "Kinda... shitty you're go-ing to see me die," she says, almost too quietly to hear.

"You're not dying!" I snap before I can think better of it. Her body jerks from the sound, and she cries out in pain. "Fuck. Sorry." I wince.

Joe gives me a hard look, telling me to get my shit together.

"You're not dying," I say again, quieter this time, and she whimpers.

"Please," she almost begs.

"What?" I ask. "What do you need?"

"Let me go."

The fuck? She's seventeen, almost eighteen. She shouldn't want to die. What the hell are we missing here?

"Come on, Abbs. You're strong enough to fight through the pain. The ambulance will be here soon," I tell her, my heart racing as I try to figure out what's going on.

"Hurts," she groans. She still hasn't opened her eyes, and it's worrying me.

"Abby, sweetness, can you open your eyes and look at me? Just for a second." I wait to see what she will do. When she complies, I'm not prepared for the defeat and pain reflecting back at me from her baby blues. "Oh, baby. Whatever it is, we'll fix it. I promise," I whisper.

She looks at me with doubt before her eyes flutter shut as the sirens come into earshot.

"Call the sheriff and Doctor Evans. Tell them what happened and to meet us at the hospital. Evans may not be able to, though. Actually, just call Travis for now," I tell Joe as the red and blue lights flood the area around us.

Everything is a blur after that. The paramedics

push us aside, asking her questions she can't seem to answer. They ask us if we hit her, which instantly sends me into a rage, and Joe has to pull me away from them before I do something stupid like beat their heads in.

"Ignore it. They're just running through all of the possibilities, and doing their jobs. Which, in case you've forgotten, is to keep her alive," he reminds me. "Knowing what happened could help."

I take a deep breath to centre myself before handing him the keys to the truck. "I'm going with her. You follow us. Call Carl and Trent as well. I think Rina and Abigail have become friends of some sort," I tell him, watching the paramedics brace her neck.

Fuck. Is her neck broken? What the fuck happened to her?

"Anything else I can do?" he asks. "Maybe call her father?"

Abigail lets out a pained cry in that moment, and suddenly, I don't want that man anywhere near her. Not until we have answers.

"No, let Travis do that. He's the sheriff. It's his job," I say coldly, turning to look at my brother.

He's watching Abigail with the same intensity I'm feeling. The paramedics may think that was a cry of pain, and it was, but not physical pain. That was straight fear. We know that type of cry because Lana makes the same sound when she has one of her flashbacks or nightmares.

Until we have more answers, I'm not letting her out of my sight and the mayor is getting nowhere near her.

# CHAPTER 5
# DAMEON

"SIR, WE NEED YOU TO WAIT OUT HERE," A VOICE TELLS me, but I can't focus.

The entire ride in the ambulance was a blur as we left Haven Hills and drove to the nearest hospital, almost an hour away. Abigail stopped breathing once, and I thought I was going to be sick. I am grateful they were able to bring her back.

"No," I growl. "I'm not going anywhere."

"Sir. You don't have a choice. Step back, or I will have security escort you out. We can't help her if you're fighting with us."

The nurse in front of me comes into focus. She's wearing Winnie the Pooh scrubs and sporting a seriously stern face. She's probably in her early fifties, if I had to guess, and I guarantee she's seen some shit.

Even now, there's blood on her uniform. Probably Abigail's.

Fuck.

"I've got him, Thelma. Go help her," Travis says behind me.

She gives him a long look before nodding and turning on her heel to walk through the double doors where they took Abigail. When I try to follow, a large hand grabs my shoulder like a vise, holding me in place.

"No way. You heard what she said. Abby needs them to be focused on her, and you need to brief me on what happened because I can't fathom how that little girl almost died tonight," Travis says, making me stiffen.

"She's not dying," I growl, turning on him. He doesn't move away from me in fear like most would on instinct alone.

Then again, the sheriff has been through some shit in his life. Haven Hills used to be a quiet little town where nothing ever went wrong. But with my sister's ex stalking and kidnapping her, followed by his woman's father trying to kill her, he's seen too much recently.

Now Abigail being found broken and bleeding

on the side of the road, just outside of town limits? Yeah, it's a lot to fucking deal with.

"Let's hope not." He guides me into a smaller waiting room, where Joe is already sitting with Trent. "Take a seat," he says, waving his hand at the couch where my brother is sitting before joining Trent on another couch across from us.

Trent has been working with Travis for a while. After Lana came back home, he was intent on keeping her safe when her abusive ex was granted bail and disappeared.

They had butted heads at first, given that Trent didn't tell him he was in town. Being a detective with the Omaha Police Department, our good sheriff assumed he would have been notified the moment another city was operating in his town. But Trent was technically on leave and his only focus was Lana.

They obviously worked through their issues eventually.

"Walk us through tonight from the beginning," Trent says, looking between Joe and me.

I'm sure my brother has already told him every-thing, but he needs to fact check. Even if he trusts us and is about to become our brother-in-law, it's his job.

"Please," Travis adds in.

I nod. "We were on our way home from *Ignition*. I was talking to Joe about some... brotherly things." I wince. Definitely not something I want to be made public knowledge.

"Alright. What happened next?" Trent asks, moving on before Travis could dig deeper into that conversation. I'm not sure he would have, but I'm grateful all the same.

"I was lost in my thoughts when he yelled to stop, and I slammed on the brakes." I shiver, still hearing the panic in his voice. "Joe was already out of the truck before I could ask him what was wrong. The moment I saw him leaning over something, I got out too."

"I knew it was Abigail before I got to her. In the dark, I wasn't exactly positive it was a human, but I wasn't discounting it either, so I made him stop," Joe explains.

It takes everything in me not to hit him. Wasn't certain she was human? Though, thinking back, I wasn't sure either, until I got closer to her.

"She was already in the condition you found her?" Travis asks, and I swear, if he wasn't the sheriff, I'd deck him. I've had just about enough of people asking that question.

"She was," Joe cuts in, resting his hand on my arm to remind me to breathe. "She wasn't showing signs of consciousness until Dameon spoke to her."

I take a deep breath before telling the rest. "Her words were broken, and her breathing was erratic, but she was conscious enough to respond. But she wouldn't open her eyes until just before the ambulances arrived."

"Did she say anything about what happened to her?" Trent questions us, and we shake our heads.

"No, but when Joe mentioned calling her father, she cried out in fear," I tell them.

"How do you know it was fear rather than pain?" Travis asks.

I look between him and Trent before staying on Trent. "Because the cry was the same as Lana's when she's having a nightmare or flashback."

Travis curses as Trent swallows, darkness clouding his face.

"Has anyone notified her father?" Joe asks, and Travis sighs.

"I sent Ethan over there, but he's not ho—" His phone ringing cuts him off.

"Yeah? Report," he says briskly into his phone, and I sit up straighter. It has to be Ethan. He's the only other deputy that works at the station with him and Trent.

"Yeah. Take him into holding until he sobers up. We'll figure out where to go from there." Travis slams his phone on the table, sitting back down, looking confused.

"You found him?" Trent asks what we're all asking.

"Ethan did." He nods. "A neighbour found him passed out in their yard, with dishevelled clothing." He looks between the three of us warily. "We can't know for certain what happened tonight until Abigail wakes up and can talk to us, or he sobers up. Though right now, I'm not sure I will believe what he says."

"Why?" Joe asks, sounding as confused as I feel. Travis is always one to uphold the law of innocent until proven guilty, so him saying this is out of character.

He pinches the bridge of his nose, his hand shaking before it drops back into his lap. "Because his knuckles are bruised, and he's got blood on him. From what Ethan can tell, he's not injured, so it can't be his."

That son of a bitch. Mayor or not, I'm going to kill him.

"Sheriff," the nurse, Thelma, calls out as she walks into the room.

Glancing at my watch, I can't believe we've already been in here for an hour. I jump up, ready to ask her a million questions, when Travis stands in front of me.

"What is it?" he asks.

"We've done the necessary x-rays and MRI," she explains, her voice sounding harsh. "When we cleaned her up, we also discovered she has bruising wrapping around her neck. It's evident she's been strangled with an object of some kind."

"Is she going to survive?" Travis asks.

Trent leans over to whisper into my ear before I can say anything. "You can't be the one to ask right now, man. She can't legally answer you, but she can answer the sheriff," he explains, and the tension leaves my shoulders a bit.

He's right. I hadn't thought that far ahead, too consumed with the panic and fear of her not surviving this.

"She has a long recovery ahead of her. She has a concussion, three broken ribs, and a lot of deep bruising around her middle," she says quietly. "But there's something else you should know."

"What is it?" Travis asks, his body bracing for whatever she's about to tell him.

When I look around him at the nurse, she looks angry and sad. I don't like it at all. I just know this is going to be bad.

"It's late, and Abigail has extensive injuries, so clearly she is our top priority at the moment." She takes a deep breath. "The x-rays show that there's evidence of continued abuse over the span of years. Breaks that have healed, scar tissue. You name it, there's evidence of it. We'd need to run more tests to get a better idea, but the doctor needs parental consent as she's not yet eighteen."

"Her father is currently in a holding cell in Haven Hills," Travis tells her, his voice cool and deadly. "He's extremely inebriated, and his hands are bruised with some blood on his clothing. He's not useful right now."

"Are you calling it, then, Sheriff?"

He nods. "I'm making this an official investigation. Mayor Davies is being investigated for childhood abuse and attempted murder. Do what you need to."

Attempted.

Fucking.

Murder.

# CHAPTER 6
## ABIGAIL

STARTLING AWAKE, I GASP FOR BREATH AS MY HANDS fly to my throat. My body screams in pain from the fast movements, causing me to cry out in pain.

"Hey, it's okay. You're okay," I hear Rose say beside me, clearing the fog of panic. Her soft and familiar features calming me.

Another nightmare. Just fucking great. I'm getting real tired of this shit, and fast. I have no outlet while I'm in here, and I've already had to talk to a psychiatrist about my way of coping.

When I first woke up in the hospital three days ago, the sheriff and Dameon were sitting in my room and had told me I'd been out for over twenty-four hours. They asked me questions about that night, but not before telling me that my father had been arrested for attempted murder as well as continued child abuse. Apparently, my x-rays and other tests gave up all my secrets while I was unconscious.

"Rose," I whisper, slowly lowering myself back to the pillows with her help. "Fuck. I hate this," I say quietly, trying to fight off the tears.

"I'm so sorry, babe. I hate this for you, but I'm not sorry that bastard is rotting in a jail cell," she spits out, making me chuckle. Not because it's funny, but because she's never been one to get heated. That's usually reserved for me.

"I still can't believe they denied him bail," I admit, taking the cup of water she hands me. Isn't it almost unheard of to keep someone as prominent as him in jail?

"Yep, and I'm glad they damn well did. He deserves nothing less, babe. You never talked about it, but I knew it was worse than you ever let on," she says, tears building in her eyes. "I should have said something to someone."

I shake my head slowly, careful not to make this constant headache worse. Concussions fucking suck, but this is by far the worst one I've dealt with.

"No. This isn't on you. It's on him. No one would have believed you if you'd said what you suspected."

I sigh. "I don't think they would have believed me either."

"The tests don't lie," she says, and I give a sad smile.

"I'm not sure I would have been given the option to have those tests if I hadn't wound up here," I admit.

"I hate him, Abigail. I hate that he's done this to you, and I hate that his evil ways has affected the entire town." Rose shakes her head. She's referring to the fact that Dad's abuse and attempted murder of me has left the entire mayoral office under investigation. It's left a dark stain on Haven Hills' history, and Sheriff Colt is the one that has to clean it up.

"Oh, Dameon was here a while ago. He wants to see you," Rose says, changing the subject with a smirk.

Fuck.

Of all the people that could have found me, it had to be him? And even though my memory is a bit fuzzy, I know for a fact I begged him to let me die. It's probably what he wants to talk about.

Unless he knows the real reason behind the bandage on my forearm. But that can't be it, right? I never said a word, and the doctors are sworn to confidentiality.

After my first meeting with Dr. Patrick—an out of town psychiatrist—where I promised I wasn't suicidal and death wasn't the motivation behind the cutting, he promised not to tell anyone as long as I agreed to continue treatment.

I think the sheriff is aware since I haven't turned eighteen yet, but he wouldn't have told anyone, right?

"How long ago was a while?" I ask, my heart racing from the endless possibilities of what he may want to talk about.

The machine beside me starts beeping faster, alerting to my panicked state, and Rose's eyes widen.

"I think like an hour ago? You need to breathe, babe. Take a deep breath," she instructs, guiding me through some breaths until the beeping slows down.

"What's going on here?" The nurse walks into my room, looking between the two of us as she comes to listen to my heart.

Thelma is nice. Apparently, she was the nurse on call the night I was brought in.

"I told her Dameon is here wanting to talk to her, and she panicked," Rose explains.

Thelma looks at me, her eyes softening. "As much as that man is a royal pain in my ass, you don't have to fear him." She gives me a knowing look. "He only knows what you have given us and the sheriff permission to tell him."

Letting out a deep breath and relaxing into the bed, I smile up at her. "Thank you."

She nods, removing the stethoscope and checking my vitals. "How is your pain? You're due for another round of pain medication if you need it."

"Yes please. But nothing stronger than ibuprofen," I remind her, and she snorts.

"You may just be the toughest, most stubborn patient I have ever met. Most people that have been through what you have would welcome the stronger stuff. But, alright, I will get the script written up from the doctor."

I give a sad smile, acknowledging her concern. "I know. Thank you."

Truth is, the idea of anything stronger scares me. It would take me away from my problems and shut my brain off. Just like the cutting does, but for a much longer period of time. That escape is something I could easily become addicted to, and I can't take that chance.

"When it gets here, I'll bring it in with some orange juice. Your sugar is a bit on the low side, and I'd like to get it back up," she says, finishing up whatever she has to do. I don't really understand the charts, and I'm not sure I want to. I know what the doctors have told me and that's enough.

I nod my head, grateful to have their help. "Thank you."

Once she leaves the room, Rose moves to the side of my bed again, raising an eyebrow. "Something you didn't tell me?"

I swallow the thick emotion down, nodding. "Yes, but it's not something I'm ready for others to know right now," I tell her, picking at the fibres of the blanket placed over my legs.

I'm not ready for the pity and possible shame others will show when they find out I self-harm as a coping mechanism. Nor the judgement and stigma that goes along with it.

I'm not suicidal, and that's something too many people believe about people who self-harm. While some are, there are others like myself who don't want to die. We just can't find another way to regulate our thoughts and emotions.

It's a coping mechanism. Not an attempt to exit life.

The psychiatrist has already given me some ideas and tools to try when I'm feeling overwhelmed. So far, the only one I've been able to try is snapping a rubber band against my wrist, but it seems to help a bit.

"I'm here whenever you need to talk. You know that, right?" Rose says.

"I know, and I'm so lucky to have you as a best friend. I don't know what I did to deserve you, but I'm sure as hell not letting you go."

"Shut up," she says through tears of her own.

Mine have started to fall freely now, but I don't care. I mean every word I said. She's my best friend and my rock, and I'd be lost without her.

"I love you," I say, smirking.

"I love you, too." She wipes at her cheeks to remove the tears before clearing her throat. "Now, first order of business." A sternness overtakes her, and suddenly I want to giggle.

"Uh-oh, Rosie has her serious face on," I tease, and she rolls her eyes.

"Where are you going to stay when they release you next week?"

Her question makes my stomach drop. The topic of where I'm going to live has been on my mind since I woke up in the hospital, but I hate thinking about it. I know her parents have offered to let me move in with them until I can get settled on my own two feet, but I can't let them do that. I don't want to be a burden to anyone. And hiding from the police for a couple of weeks—my original plan when I left the house that night—is no longer an option.

"That's where we come in," the sheriff says from the door, making me jump, then groan. "Sorry. I should have knocked." He winces, taking in the hand on my stomach.

"It's fine," I tell him before moving my eyes to the man standing beside him.

It's none other than Dameon Easton.

# CHAPTER 7
# ABIGAIL

"I think I'm going to get back to the school before free period is over," Rose says quietly, leaning down to hug me gently.

She always has a free period after her lunch, so she's been using her mom's car to drive down here and visit every day since I arrived. I love this girl so damn much, but most of the time I feel like I don't deserve her friendship.

"Okay. Drive safe," I reply quietly.

"I will, babe. Promise." She gives me one last look. "I'm going to try to get you a phone before I come back tomorrow. I miss talking to you." She acknowledges the sheriff and Dameon, nodding to them on her way out.

Once she's gone, the sheriff closes the door and pulls a chair to the side of the bed.

"How are you feeling, Abigail?" he asks gently. It isn't often I spend time around him, but he's always seemed like a stern man.

Rina, his fiancé and my friend, loves the heck out of him. I often find myself a little jealous of them. I want their type of love one day. I can't help but admire how adorable it is to watch his eyes soften every time he looks at her.

"I'm okay." It's not an outright lie. I could be a lot worse off right now, so I'm counting my blessings.

"Your pain? Have you been taking your medication?" Dameon asks in a curt tone that has me rolling my eyes, and Sheriff Colt sighing.

"Not your business," he warns D.

"It is when she's coming to live with me," D countered.

Wait, what?

"Live with you? Me? Are you high?" I squeak out, wondering what the fuck he's talking about.

He just laughs a little, and then the sheriff's words come back to me.

"What did you mean when you said that was where you came in, Sheriff Colt?" I questioned, turning my head to look at him.

"Call me Travis," he orders, and I wiggle in the bed a little. The idea of calling him by his first name just feels weird to me.

"Hmm." Dameon makes a little noise, but Sheri — Travis, speaks before I can look over.

"You're friends with Rina," he states, and I nod. "Has she told you anything about Serenity Stables and our goal for it? The reasons behind all of the upgrades that have been made recently?" he asks, waiting patiently for my response. The man has a lot more patience than the grumbling dummy on the other side of my bed.

"The whole secret mission thing?" I ask, not wanting to get Rina in trouble for saying anything. I'm not sure how much I'm supposed to know, exactly.

They both bark out a laugh.

"We're not spies, sweetness," Dameon says with another chuckle.

"Speak for yourself. I think our mission is pretty secret and badass," Travis says, winking at me.

Okay, that's nice.

"True, it is," Dameon concurs.

"Anyway, yes. In a sense it is a secret, but not from most of the people involved in some capacity. Rina included, and I trust her judgement. If she told you what we were doing, I know I can trust you because she does."

That leaves a pit of guilt in my tummy. Trust. That's something I don't have a lot of, given my upbringing. Not to mention the fact that I've literally lied to everyone by omission for years. He shouldn't trust me at all.

"Oh, no you don't," Dameon growls, causing me to jump. "Stop thinking whatever you were thinking about that put this sad look on your face."

Sheesh. Can't a girl keep a secret anymore?

*Yeah, like that's worked out so well for you. Look where you are, Abby.*

Ugh, stupid inner monologue, conscience thing.

"You're not exactly the boss of me. You know that, right?" I say to him, deciding to be stern rather than think about my feelings.

He smiles down at me, making me grind my teeth in annoyance. Ass.

"You sure about that, Abbs?" He keeps smiling.

Sh—Travis clears his throat. "You know that we chose to turn it from a family ranch into somewhat of a witness protection safe house, then?" he asks, getting back to the topic at hand, and I nod.

"Yeah. It's actually really cool. Pretty smart too, but what does that have to do with me?" I ask, not following. Not that this headache is helping my ability to think any.

Someone knocks on the door before pushing it open. Thelma walks in carrying a tray with a medicine cup and orange juice. When she greets Travis respectfully before scowling at Dameon, it takes everything in me not to laugh.

"I see you have some more company," she says, moving to the side of the bed D is on and forcing him out of the way.

"I'm popular today," I say jokingly, making her smile again.

D is still staring at her with a scowl of his own, clearly not enjoying being pushed aside. Too bad, my dude.

"I have the ibuprofen you requested, as well as a couple of regular strength Tylenol," she says, handing me the medicine cup.

"Why both?" I ask.

"Because the doctor on call asked me how you were doing, and I told him you were squinting a lot. He would prefer you take something a little stronger, but we're respecting your wishes," she tells me.

"Thank you. This won't do anything to me? Taking them both at once, I mean."

"Not at all. It might make you a little tired, but

that will be because the pain will be easing up, allowing your body to relax," she explains, and I nod.

"Okay."

She waits for me to toss the pills into my mouth, then hands me the glass of orange juice to help bring my sugar levels back up.

"Should she be drinking sugar if she has a migraine?" Dameon questions.

Thelma doesn't even turn to look at him. Like she said earlier, she won't tell him anything without my or Travis' consent.

"You can explain this," I tell her after I've taken the pain meds.

Thelma turns to the guys while I rest my head against the pillow, the energy draining from me. I am so tired. I know it isn't the pills, but I feel like I've been running a marathon for days with no break. Healing always sucks so much.

"Her sugars are low, which could also be contributing to the migraine she has. We use orange juice as a natural way to elevate the levels without medication."

Dameon looks confused. "Is she diabetic? Does she need medication?" he asks, and I groan.

"I'm not diabetic," I say tiredly.

"No, she's not. But her body has been put through the wringer and is recovering from trauma, as you know. That level of recovery saps a lot of energy from one's system." She turns to Travis. "If you could grab her whatever food she tells you is her favourite craving right now, it will likely help. If it's something Abigail loves, she will probably be able to eat more than a few bites." She pauses. "Healthy food, of course," she adds on.

"Of course." Travis nods.

I feel myself yawning as she leaves us alone, and Dameon looks me over, frowning.

"You need to get some sleep. We'll come back and talk about all of this once you've gotten some rest and you're in less pain," he dictates like his word is law.

I want to argue with him, but I just don't have it in me. I'm tired and in too much pain. Sleep sounds amazing right now.

"That sounds like a good plan," Travis says, looking at me. "What's your favourite food? And some snacks I can bring that don't need to be refrigerated?"

I sigh. I feel bad that the man has had to become my official guardian for the next couple of weeks. While he's told the hospital that I am able to make decisions regarding my health, as long as it doesn't put me in danger of something, it must suck being stuck with a kid you barely know.

"Umm, I don't know. Maybe a cheeseburger with a Caesar salad?" I ask, hoping the salad will be excuse enough to get the gooey, greasy goodness of a cheeseburger.

"I shouldn't get you the cheeseburger," he says, looking thoughtful. "But if you promise to eat at least half of the salad before touching the burger, you have a deal."

Tough sale, dude. So mean. I just want my yummy food, but I do like my salads too.

"Deal."

## CHAPTER 8
## DAMEON

ABIGAIL BETTER BE GETTING SOME SLEEP RIGHT NOW. And what the hell was that caregiver shit Travis was trying to pull back there? She's not his little or his sub, so what the fuck?

"She shouldn't be eating a cheeseburger," I say from the passenger side of his truck.

"Her sugars are low. If she's not eating, then she can't heal. It was a bargain worth making to ensure she finally eats something instead of picking at it," he says in a stern voice.

Fine. He has a point. But I would rather she ate something healthier in order to bring her energy back up.

"Why couldn't her favourite food be something

like a spinach, kale, and banana smoothie?" I ask, sighing and leaning back against the seat.

He barks out a laugh. "If you think any little or middle is going to request that over a cheeseburger, you may need to have your head examined."

I frown. "You think she's into age play?" I ask.

Clearly there are some signs, but I just attributed them to her age rather than the possibility of being a little. I can't be a Daddy. It's just not my thing.

*And why are you even thinking you'd be her Daddy, anyway, idiot? You said you don't like her that way.*

*Shut up, conscience. I don't need you.*

"I think it's a very strong possibility, but not age play. I think Abigail probably regresses from trauma. It's not overly noticeable since she's still a teenager, but it's there," he explains as we head back to the hospital.

"How do you mean? Lana regresses," I muse, and he nods.

"Lana and Pixie both do. But they also age play to an extent. I don't think Abby is the same way."

Everyone and their cutesie names for each other. It's annoyingly sappy when you're the odd one out in said group.

Trent calls my sister sweet pea. Travis calls Katrina, his woman, Pixie. I'm sure it's only a matter of time before Joe and Carl find someone too at this rate.

*You did call Abby sweetness earlier. And you call Lana Firecracker.*

I guess I'm a sucker for sweet nicknames after all.

"Are you sure you want to be the one to watch over her?" Travis pulls me out of my head, and I scowl.

"Wouldn't have agreed to it if I didn't want to," I point out. "And we both know Serenity is the safest place for her."

He gives me a dry look. "Mayor Davies is in jail, and there is no one in this town willing to give him bail. She's completely safe wherever she chooses to go. Rina and I would be happy to help her get back on her feet," he tells me, and I want to clock him.

"You remember the other reason Lana wanted Serenity to become public, right?" I question.

"To keep people safe. Because it was healing for your family to be near horses," he says, nodding in understanding.

"It's more than that, though." I sigh, trying to sort through the thoughts in my mind. "When that prick beat Lana, she didn't feel safe in the city. Hell, she didn't feel safe here, either. But she felt protected with us around her, because she knew we would do whatever it took to protect her."

"Yes, but Abigail doesn't have that connection with you," he reminds me.

"Maybe not, but the thing that helped Lana most was Cocoa. Being able to take care of her horse, rebuilding that connection, was crucial for her mental health. Especially when the therapists were useless before Derek came along," I explain.

Derek is Travis' brother, and works as a psychiatrist in Kansas. When Lana started talking with him, we could all take a breath because we began seeing little pieces of our sister come back to us. Now, Derek is working with Serenity remotely for any clients who need not only the protection we offer, but someone to talk to that they could trust.

"Derek is great like that. He's helped Rina a lot too after everything her father and ex put her through," he says absentmindedly.

He's been struggling to accept what happened to Katrina when her father kidnapped her along with Lana. He'd beaten her so badly she barely survived it, and he's trying to work through the self-blame stage. Which I completely understand.

I nod. "He's a good guy for sure. Getting back on topic, though. Horses are sentient animals. They are very healing and compassionate to humans when they feel safe around. I think with everything that Abby's father has done to her, being near the horses, and on a very secure ranch, will do her a lot of good."

He looks impressed at the fierceness in my voice, but I'm passionate about the ranch. It's our family's legacy, and it saved not only my mother, but Joe and Lana as well.

If we can share that healing with others while keeping them safe, I know it would make our parents proud. They may no longer be alive, but we're carrying on the legacy that Dad had started when he built the ranch for our mother's bipolar disorder.

"Alright," he agrees. When he turns into the driveway of the hospital and parks the car, he turns to look at me. "But if she says no, you have to accept that. Are you able to do that?" he asks, and I close my eyes.

"I can," I tell him, knowing she won't. Lana is already on her way to talk to Abby about Serenity Stables when she wakes up. If anyone can sell Abby on the importance of the ranch, it's my sister.

"Right." He watches me for a moment. "You have something planned."

I smile. "Lana is coming to visit her while she eats."

Travis blows out a breath before getting out of the truck, taking Abigail's food with him. "You better hope that doesn't upset her. Thelma is like a mother hen with her. If anyone upsets Abby, she's liable to kick our asses before kicking us out."

Yeah, not a fucking chance. I would never do anything to make Abigail more upset than she already is. Seems to me she's been through more than enough for a lifetime. I'm not about to be the one to cause her any more pain.

# CHAPTER 9
## ABIGAIL

"YOU ARE A LITERAL GOD!" I SHOUT, GRABBING THE bag of yummy goodness Travis hands me. I will never call him Sheriff again if it means I get gooey, greasy food delivery.

*Okay, Abby, grow up. You're almost eighteen, and this is not how you're supposed to act.*

"Remember to eat the salad before the burger," he says in a stern voice, being a total killjoy.

Ugh. I like salad, I do, but the burger just smells so good!

"Do I have to?" I whine, deciding I'm in the mood to pull the injured and whiny card.

"Technically, I can't make you," he begins, just as Dameon scoffs. Travis gives him a look before turning back to me. "But you don't seem like the type of person to go back on their word. Are you, Abby?"

Darn him and his logic. Of course I'm not. I huff out a breath and pull the salad out first.

The giant smile he gives me makes me feel like a million bucks. I don't know why. I guess maybe it's because he seems like he could actually be proud of me, and I haven't had a lot of that.

"Good girl," Dameon says in a deep voice that sends a zing of pleasure through me.

*Nope. No way, Abigail. He likes things you have no business even thinking about. You've heard the rumours, and that's not something you want. Even if he does it all in pleasure, there's no way you can ever handle that.*

*So, you're going to pretend his praise didn't just affect you and make you tingle all over, and glare at him instead, then?* Ah, there's that deep look of frustration and annoyance he usually wears around me. Much better.

"Knock, knock," someone says from the door before she enters into the room with a big man behind her.

There's such a contrast between them that I'm momentarily speechless. I knew Lana was back in town and had been for a while, but she doesn't like to leave the ranch much, so I haven't really seen her. She looks good... and happy. Lucky her.

The man behind her is tall and muscular with a peppered beard. I know him because he works with Travis at the Sheriff's Department and has been to the hospital a couple of times already. Trent, I believe his name is. He's a scary looking mother-fucker. I might be afraid of him being in my room right now if he wasn't looking at Lana like she was the most precious thing on this earth. Someone who looks at a woman like that can't be scary. Right?

"Hey, firecracker," Dameon greets her, pulling her in for a hug and kissing the top of her head.

My chest constricts a little as an unfamiliar feeling washes over me.

"Hey," she says when she pulls back before turning to look at me. "Hi, Abby. I'm not sure you remember me," she starts, and I nod as I shovel a forkful of salad into my mouth.

God, that's so good. Nevermind, the gooey deliciousness can wait.

"I remember," I tell her once I've swallowed the salad down.

She smiles at me, waving her hand at the chair beside the bed, asking for permission to sit which is super sweet of her. When I nod, she sits down and Travis clears his throat.

"Dameon and I are going to leave you to eat, Abby, but we'd like to talk to you after?" he asks, and I snort.

It's definitely not a question, but at least he was polite enough to word it as one.

"Sure, Sheriff." I roll my eyes, and he smirks.

"Eat the salad first." He points his finger at me before walking out the door.

Dameon stops and looks from Lana to me. "Promise me something, sweetness," he says, pleading with me for something I'm not even aware of.

"W-what?" My throat feels dry as I try and speak.

"Really listen to her, okay?" He watches me, and I frown. Why wouldn't I listen to her? She seems nice.

"Of course," I promise him. The second the words pass my lips, I notice the tension leaving his shoulders. After a moment, dips his head in thanks and leaves us alone, closing the door behind him.

"He's such a worrywart," Lana says, drawing my attention to her.

"He's worried about you?" I ask, wondering why. Not that it's any of my business, but I ask her anyway. "Are you okay?"

She giggles. "Oh, I'm fine! If I weren't, Trent never would have left the room." She waves her hand to dismiss that notion, like he's just an overprotective brute.

"He's like... intense," I say after taking a few more bites of salad. Being around her is surprisingly calming. It makes sense to me why her and Rina are best friends.

"He can be. Did Rina tell you about the first time she met him?" Lana asks, giggling to herself while I shake my head and take another couple of bites of salad. It's almost gone, and then I get the best part of this meal.

"She tried to protect me from him. From behind the bars of the cell she was in down at the station," she says, giggling again.

Right. I'd forgotten our good sheriff had arrested her before he fell in love with her.

"She tried to protect you from Trent?" I ask, dumbfounded. I don't think that man would never hurt a woman, but especially not Lana.

She nods. "She didn't have very good experiences with men before Travis," she says quietly, the mood shifting with that one statement.

I swallow down the sadness inside of me, refusing to let it surface right now. Seems like women fearing men is an all too common occurrence after all. Men too, I'm sure, we just don't hear about it nearly as often.

"I get that," I tell her while pulling the cheeseburger out of the bag and unwrapping it.

This conversation is starting to get heavy, and I have a feeling it's about to get worse I completely refuse to let this burger go to waste either, so... and maybe nurse Thelma will stop hounding on me now that I've finally eaten something.

"Yum! That looks delicious!" Lana says as she eyes my burger. I'm not sharing. Nope. Mine.

"It's a bribe to make me eat." I shrug, taking a bite and moaning. "So good."

"Da—Trent will do that with me sometimes too," she says, correcting herself.

I know Travis and Rina's dynamic, but Rina would never talk about someone else, so I didn't know if Lana was the same or not, but I suspected as much.

When Rina first confided in me, I did a lot of research on it to try and understand my new friend. I can honestly say the idea of age regression is solid, and I can see the appeal of wanting to be younger... even needing to be.

I doubt it would ever be for me, but I would never judge someone else either. My issue is within my own brain. I'd kill to be able to regress, I just have no clue how.

"It's sneaky. But really, I'm totally coming out the winner in this scenario," I tell her around a mouthful of burger.

"Oh, totally. You're lucky it wasn't Dameon that got the guardianship over you. He's a hardass when it comes to health." She sighs, shaking her head. "He's super into needing to eat three solid meals a day with lots of snacks, and it's totally unnatural."

I laugh hard, gasping when my ribs protest in pain. "Shit." Groaning, I rest my burger on the table thing placed over my lap.

"Ah crap!" Lana winces, standing. "Can I help? I'm sorry, I didn't mean to make you laugh."

Through the pain, I almost want to laugh again. She's fucking adorable. "No, it's fine. It's my fault for forgetting I'm beaten up at the moment," I say, trying to use dark humour to ease her.

"I'm sorry you had to go through what you did," she says quietly, and I sober up.

"It's okay. It's behind me now, right?" I say quietly, matching her tone and demeanour. It will never be okay, but I have to live with it so I'll figure it out.

"Hey, do you like horses?" Lana asks, shocking me with the abrupt change in conversation.

Why do I feel like there's a lot more meaning behind that seemingly simple question?

## CHAPTER 10
## DAMEON

"Do you think she'll be successful in convincing her?" Travis asks Trent as I try not to pace the floor.

I really fucking hope Lana can convince Abby to move out to Serenity. She'll be safe and cared for there, and I'll be able to keep a close eye on her while she's recovering from both the physical and mental aspects of what has happened to her.

"Of course. This is Lana's passion, and once she tells Abigail her own story of survival, I think it will be a done deal," Trent reassures our good sheriff.

"There are things that Abigail is going through that Lana hasn't," I say, shaking my head. "We need to keep a very close eye on her."

Travis nods in agreement. "You will. I'm sure all of you will be watching out for her," he states.

"No one is going to hurt her again," I vow.

"Man, you need to sit down," Trent tells me gruffly. When I don't listen, his voice gets darker. "If Lana comes out and sees you like this, it's going to upset her, brother. Sit. Down."

Damn him for saying the one thing that would make me do just about anything. My sister has been through way too much in the past year, and I refuse to be the one to cause her stress.

Shooting the asshole a glare, I take a seat across from them in the waiting room.

"Fucking finally. Do you know how on edge he's been today?" Travis jokes to Trent. "He tried to give me shit for getting her a burger."

Trent frowns. "Should she be eating a burger right now? That's not overly healthy unless they're made at home from scratch."

"Thank you!" I all but shout, glad that someone sees my side of things here.

Travis rolls his eyes at my antics, but I don't give a fuck. I like being told I'm right, even if it's in a round-about way.

"Normally, I would agree. But like I told your brother-in-law over there, her sugars are extremely low. Right now, our only focus is to get them back up, and she needs to eat for that. If a cheeseburger is what makes her eat, then so be it." He shrugs. "Besides, I made her eat a salad first before she could touch the burger. It's a win."

"I suppose the pros do outweigh the cons in this scenario. I wouldn't go making a habit of feeding her junk, though," Trent directs at me.

"Yes, because I have so much junk food at my place. Believe me, I know what I'm doing." I cross my arms over my chest and take a deep breath.

"There's something you aren't telling me," my astute brother to be surmises.

"You don't get it, Trent. Seeing her like that when we found her? Christ! She begged me to let her die, man," I say quietly, my chest tightening.

She's not even eighteen for a couple more weeks, yet she told me to let her die with so much conviction in her voice. It's not normal for someone so young to just want it all to end.

His eyes soften as understanding dawns on him. "You're protective over her." I nod. "You have feelings for her."

I scowl at him, making the two of them smirk like they're in on some grand secret.

"Now isn't the time to be thinking about any of that shit," I say defensively.

"It's just a statement of fact, man. Relax." Trent is calm as always, but I can see the look in his eyes.

If anyone is going to understand my reservations about caring for and feeling attracted to someone I watched grow up, it's him. Only, I never knew Abigail as anything other than a kid in town. She was never close to our family, and I kind of get why now.

"Has the bastard confessed yet?" I ask, changing the topic.

"The evidence is stacked against him. He knows there's no denying what he's put her through." Travis' face is dark as he speaks, and I'm right there with him.

"He deserves to be tortured in the same way he hurt her. Sitting in a jail cell for the rest of his life is getting off easy if you ask me," I growl out. "No one deserves the shit he did to her, and she was a fucking kid."

"That's a contradictory statement," Travis points out how illogical I'm being. "But I get where you're coming from."

"Lana's coming out," Trent tells us, standing and putting his phone away.

I stand with him, waiting to see if I can read her face when she walks around the corner, but she only has eyes for Trent. She walks into his arms, giving him a tight squeeze and taking a deep breath before relaxing.

"You okay, sweet pea?" he asks her, and she pulls away to smile up at him.

God, the love they have for one another is deep and intense. I'm so fucking happy my little sister has that type of love in her life, but damn if I don't kind of want it for myself too.

"I'm good. It was just a lot, going over everything that happened with Ryan. I didn't tell her about Rina's father because it's not fully my story to tell. She also doesn't need to hear about everything bad happening in the world while horrible things were being done to her."

He nods and looks over at me, and her eyes follow. When she sees me, her face breaks into a giant smile. "She's agreed to come to Serenity when she's released... but I promised to help her spend time with the horses." She blushes a bit. "I also volunteered for you to teach her how to ride when she's ready."

Trent chuckles, shaking his head. "Just going ahead and volunteering others now, huh?"

Lana shrugs. "If it means she'll come live with us

where she's safe and protected? Definitely." Can't argue with that.

"Teaching her to ride will be a piece of cake once we figure out the right horse when she's completely healed." I'm so fucking happy she agreed to come stay with me, I want to scream it from the rooftops.

"Sheriff," an older man calls out, catching our attention.

"Dr. Patrick. What can I do for you?" Travis asks him politely.

"I just stopped in to see Ms. Davies and she's told me she's moving to the ranch upon release?" he questions, and Travis nods. "Then, could you and Mr. Easton come with me please? Ms. Davies has agreed to talk."

Agreed to talk? About what?

## CHAPTER 11
## ABIGAIL

I JUST AGREED TO LIVE AT SERENITY WITH DAMEON, and now, according to the doc, I have to tell him about my coping mechanism.

"What?" I say to the empty room, trying hard to catch my breath. The doctor just left to go grab Travis and Dameon, and I'm having a hard time breathing.

I never wanted anyone to find out about the cutting, and in a matter of what feels like seconds, everyone is finding out and it's just too fucking much.

I can't catch my breath and everything feels like it's spinning out of control. When I reach to try and grab hold of something, anything to steady myself, I come up empty.

"What the hell?" someone curses, but I feel like I'm going to throw up. I can't pay attention to anything aside from what's happening with me.

I feel hands on my face, forcing me to look up, and even though it's blurry as hell, I can tell it's D. I'd recognize his annoying ass anywhere.

"I-," I suck in a breath and he curses before his hold tightens on me as he bends down to look me in the eye, squeezing my face tighter.

"Abigail Davies, you are going to breathe right the fuck now," he orders, and I almost want to roll my eyes at the bossy bastard. If I was capable of it right now, that is.

"Dameon," someone, I think Trent, says his name in a warning tone, but D's eyes never leave mine. There's something about his touch and gaze that seems to be pulling me back to reality.

"Trent, leave." It's all he says, but the firmness of his voice sends shivers down my spine and he notices. His eyes flare to life as he watches me. "Breathe, sweetness. Now."

Another order, but I do it anyway. Inhaling so sharply, I almost choke when the air hits my throat.

"Again," he says, still forcing me to look at him and only him.

With each breath I take, I feel myself calming

down a little more, my lungs burning from the lack of air, but that's nothing new. What is new is having someone to guide me through the panic this time.

"Good girl, sweetness," Dameon praises me, making my cheeks heat.

I close my eyes, trying to compose myself before facing anyone that just witnessed me in such a vulnerable state.

"Thank you," I whisper, taking another deep breath to push away the tears threatening to surface.

"Anytime, sweetness," he says, staring into my eyes for a moment before releasing his hold on me. It's odd how settled I feel when he makes no move to back away from me, but I'm not going to complain. Not right now.

"Well, it's a party in here, isn't it?" Dr. Patrick says when he steps into the room.

I offer him a weak smile. "Apparently I'm popular today," I try to joke.

It clearly falls flat but he offers me a gentle smile all the same before looking around the room. "I'm sorry, but if you're not Sheriff Colt, Mr. Easton, or Abigail, I'm going to have to ask you to leave."

Everyone nods and Lana walks over to hug Dameon before turning to me with a question on her face. Her and Trent must have come back in with the others to say a final goodbye before heading home, but the look she gives warms me. It's like she's asking for my permission to hug me even though she just gave me a hug before I freaked out.

I try and smile enough to reassure her, and after a moment's hesitation, she bends down to give me a gentle hug. "You're so strong, Abby. Remember that," she whispers into my ear before pulling away.

Well, fuck. I cannot cry, I won't.

Once everyone else has left, Dr. Patrick closes the door and turns to look at me. "Are you sure you're alright with this?" he questions, and I swallow hard.

"Yeah, I am. I just..." I trail off, but he gets it. He's been doing this a long time and isn't located in Haven Hills, so I'm sure I'm not his first cutter.

"Abigail," Travis says my name gently, drawing my attention to him. "He's not going to judge you."

"Why the hell would I judge her?" D asks, snarling like the words leave a bad taste in his mouth.

"Because I'm a fuck-up," I say under my breath, but he's close enough to hear it.

"Excuse me?" he says, whirling around to face me directly. "You did not just say what I think you just said."

"It wasn't for your ears, so I don't think I need to

repeat myself," I tell him, acting braver than I feel. It's a complete copout given this whole meeting is happening because Dameon needs to know the truth about me.

How I went from no one knowing to way too many people needing to know my business is absolutely exhausting.

"Try again, sweetness," he says, crossing his arms over his chest and staring me down.

"Maybe we should take a deep breath, Mr. Easton, and try to remember you are here because she wants you to know something," Doctor Patrick reminds him, but he doesn't budge.

"Dameon, sit down right now and listen, or I'll take Abigail home to stay with Rina and I."

Oh shit.

"Try it." D glares at him.

I sigh, feeling tired and drained from the panic attack. I just want to get this over. "I said I'm a fuck-up. Now, can you please sit down? I'd like to get through this so I can take a nap."

It's hard admitting my needs aloud, but I've been bed bound for four days. I have a long way to go before I can get back to being my normal self, so I don't really have a choice right now.

Fuck, healing is a bitch.

"We'll discuss this later," he promises, pointing a finger at me before pulling one of the chairs closer to the bed.

"Excellent," the doctor says, seeming to relax now that the giant-ass bear in the room has taken a chill-pill. "I need you to be aware of some things before Abigail can go to live with you when she's released." He looks between the three of us.

"Gathered that, doc," D snarks, and I have to fight off a smirk. Usually his attitude grates on my nerves, but right now it's lightening the situation and I'm grateful.

"Jesus, would you shut up and let the man speak?" Travis groans.

D shoots him a look like he may kick his ass later, which is a really  bad idea, but he keeps quiet and waves at the doctor to continue on.

"Mr. Easton, how much do you know about mental health and the different facets that it can entail for every scenario?"

# CHAPTER 12
# DAMEON

THAT'S A QUESTION LOADED WITH INSINUATION, NOW isn't it?

Mind you, having seen both my mother, and my brother Joe, battle bi-polar, and then Lana dealing with PTSD, I've done a lot of research into mental illness. Especially after Lana came up with the idea of helping others by making Serenity a safe space for others and not just our family.

"More than you'd think," I reply, looking at Abby with concern.

After everything she's been through the last several days, not to mention the abuse that is only now coming to light, it's not hard to see where this is going. This is going to cause severe damage mentally. It would for anyone.

"That's good," the doc replies after a moment. "Abigail, would you like to be the one to explain everything?" he asks her, and I see her stiffen on the bed.

"I uh, yeah, I guess I should," she says, swallowing hard before looking to Travis seated on the other side of her bed. When he dips his chin in encouragement, she turns her whole body to face me.

"You can trust me, Abbs. I know that doesn't seem possible for you right now, but I'm not going anywhere." I wish she could believe me, but I know it's probably way too soon for her to try and trust anyone.

Hell, it's a minor miracle she's agreed to stay with me at all instead of somewhere she knows like her friend Rose's house. Actually, that gives me an idea. I'll have to remember and track her down before Abigail is released from the hospital.

"Before I tell you anything, I need you to know I'm not suicidal," she hedges quietly.

This one statement eases my fears slightly. After she begged me to let her die the night we found her, I've been terrified she's just looking for a way out, and worried about whether or not I could help her.

"Okay," I tell her, giving her all of my attention so she knows I'm listening.

She sighs. "Dr. Patrick was called to Haven Hills because of some... injuries the hospital found." She watches me for a reaction, but I'm still confused.

I know he's not from around here. By looking him up, and seeing he's psychologist, I assumed our local doctor, Richard Evans, called him in to help her with the trauma of she's lived with.

"Of course they found injuries," Travis speaks softly to her, almost like he's speaking to a child and it feels like my heart is being squeezed in my chest.

*Mine.*

*Shit, no. Not mine, what the hell is wrong with me?*

"I know, I know," she says, shaking her head. "I just don't know how else to explain it without being looked at as though I'm pathetic or some kind of freak."

That pisses me off, but I keep it inside because she's more vulnerable right now than I have ever seen her. Right now, she's not the annoying teenager that's continually mouthing me off and giving me shit.

"Hey," I say, waiting until her eyes are on mine again. "You are neither of those things, and whatever it is that's going on, I promise you it still won't make me see you that way."

"You don't know that," she says, looking down at her hands.

"Abigail, look at me." When she shakes her head no, I lean forward in the chair and grab her hand in mine. "I'll let that pass for now, but you need to listen to me. No one here could ever think you're anything but incredibly brave and strong."

She sniffs and shakes her head, silently disagreeing with me.

"It's true, Abby," Travis says across from me.

"If you need someone to remind you, I'm more than happy to go grab nurse hard-ass to tell you otherwise. Even if she hates my very existence right now," I tell her, only half joking. That woman seems to hate me with a passion. Probably because I never leave her alone for one moment of peace while I'm here.

She giggles a little before sniffling, lifting her head to look at me. The fear I see in her beautiful blue eyes feels like a gut punch. Could she really fear me seeing her differently? I thought she hated me.

We've never been overly close, but whenever we're in the same vicinity, we just seem to piss the other one off in some way or another. So why does she look like she's about to lose me and it's the worst thing she can imagine?

Unless maybe it's just something she never wanted anyone to know.

Instead of saying another word, she rolls the sleeves of her housecoat up, revealing her forearms and holding them out to me, and it takes me a moment to see what she's trying to show me. When I do see it, my heart breaks for her.

"Sweetness," I croak, my eyes burning from the pain I feel for her. The pain I feel for the little girl that grew up abused and sought comfort in a blade, harming herself because she wanted to escape.

I've actually read a lot about self-harm because, for a while, Lana showed signs of going down that path after bringing her home. That first while before Trent came back was really hard and scary for all of us. She wouldn't talk much, she swore at us. She wasn't the Lana we remembered, so we prepared for anything.

Including this.

"Don't," she says angrily, ripping the sleeves of her robe back down to hide away the marks she's so clearly ashamed of. But she doesn't need to be. It's okay to struggle with life, and she coped in the best way she could think of. "Don't look at me with pity and barely veiled disgust."

Her words take me aback before I shake my head and narrow my eyes at her. "Pity and disgust? I think you need to read people better if that's what you think you're seeing right now, Abigail, because it's far from what I'm feeling." I match her heat with my own, holding my hand up when the doctor goes to cut in.

I'll probably catch some shit for that later, but right now, Abigail is showing the fire inside of her and I'm not about to have him interrupt us when it's the first time I've seen her this alive in days.

"Fuck you, D. Don't patronize me and tell me I need to learn to read people better. You know nothing about me!" she shouts, and I feel elated.

*Good girl. Get mad and fight. Show your strength and take your rage out on me if you need to.*

"If you think everyone is going to see you that way, then you're projecting your worst fears on us." Her nostrils flare, but I see the pain in her eyes. The truth my words touch upon. "I know it's been a long time since you've had anyone truly care for you and show compassion, but do not ever mistake those actions for pity." I shake my head. "Everyone in this room and everyone we know? We care about you and your well-being. We also think you're one of the strongest people we've ever met, so cut that shit out."

"I hate you," she says through her teeth. When the doctor moves to break us up, Travis stops him, whispering something in his ear.

"No you don't, sweetness. But if you need to pretend to hate me to keep this fire inside of you while you heal, bring it on."

"UUUGGGHHHH!" she screams in frustration. "Can you just let me have my fucking moment, Easton? Or is that too much for your damn ego to handle?" she asks, already calming down when she realizes I'm not judging her.

"You know me." I shrug. "My ego is sensitive," I say, smirking when she laughs before her face drops again.

"I'm not suicidal," she says quietly.

"I know. You said that already."

She frowns, looking confused. "You believe me?"

I nod, taking her hand in mine again and giving it a squeeze. "I told you, I know more than the doc here seems to think. My mother had bi-polar. My brother has bi-polar, and my little sister suffers from PTSD. I've done my research, Abbs."

"Mr. Easton, research isn't always enough," the

doctor tells me like I'm an idiot, so I turn to tell him everything I've ever learned about mental health.

By the time I'm done, no one in the room is questioning my ability to care for Abigail any longer. Not the sheriff, not the doctor. Not even Abby herself.

## CHAPTER 13
## ABIGAIL

I can't believe I agreed to this. It's been a week since I agreed to stay with Dameon Easton. At least, until I can find a way to support myself, and you know, turn eighteen.

This is not what I had envisioned for my immediate future. Even if it is only for a couple of months, it's still so far off of my planned path, I'm afraid following through won't be easy anymore. Everything changed when Dad almost killed me in his drunken anger.

Do I still want to leave? Yes, but I think that has more to do with my pain and fear than anything else.

Lana made a very good case for Serenity Stables

by opening up about her past trauma with her ex, though, and I know the horses have helped Rina, so why not give it a shot?

I'm not going to lie. Dameon being so knowledgeable about everything I've gone through and not judging me was a huge factor in feeling comfortable with this decision too. It also helps seeing Lana so happy even with her past of physical abuse and living PTSD. It gives me hope that I may just have a chance at feeling normal again one day.

The horses aren't a bad deal, either. I've always loved to look at them from afar. They're incredibly beautiful and majestic animals, and I can't wait to see one up close.

"Hey, you going to be okay, Abbs?" D asks me as he unlocks the door to his cabin.

The amount of security it takes to get through the gates and onto the ranch is intense. For good reason, I suppose, given it's essentially witness protection without the paper trail.

"I'm fine, D," I huff out, wincing with how harsh I sound. "Sorry."

Dr. Patrick had insisted that he be made aware of my past with cutting, so I've been on edge since then. If I thought Dameon was protective after the accident, I was barely scratching the surface. He's been staring at me non-stop since I told him the truth. He's not staring out of disgust or pity, though. Just concern.

It's an odd thing to feel when you're really not used to it. There are a lot of things I'm not used to that have become a daily occurrence since that night, but caring is definitely the biggest. I forgot what it was like to have more than your best friend truly care about you.

"It's okay to be on edge, Abbs," he says gently as he opens the door. "You've been through a lot, especially in the past couple of weeks." He closes the door behind us before turning to face me.

"What?" I ask, not able to decipher the look on his face.

"I need you to promise you'll come to me at any time, day or night, if you need someone," he tells me.

I sigh. "I will, okay? Or, I'll try at least. I'm not really used to having someone to help me, D. I'm alone."

He gets a fierce expression on his face. "You're not alone anymore, Abigail. You have people who care about you."

I nod, swallowing the thick emotion in my throat. I can't respond to that right now and he must see that because he tilts his head toward the hallway behind him.

"Come on. Let's get you settled so you can rest. You look tired."

I am tired. My ribs still ache, and doing much of anything just feels exhausting. Dad really did a number on me this time around. Thank fuck it was the last time he will ever touch me because I'm not sure I would have survived a next time.

The second he opens the door to a room further down the hall, I gasp before I can stop myself. Inside, there are items from my room like my own bedding and school books, my bookshelf with all of my novels that I refuse to apologize for. Though, knowing Dameon handled some very smutty romance novels is enough to make me blush a little.

"How?" I ask quietly, and he smiles gently, like he's proud of himself.

"That best friend of yours helped. She told us what you loved and would want to have when you were released from the hospital." He shrugs, and I make a mental note to thank Rose later. "Lana and Rina did most of the moving. None of us wanted to really touch your stuff in case it would upset you."

I swallow the emotion in my throat. God, how do people this kind exist? "Thank you," I whisper, my voice cracking.

"You're welcome."

Dameon moves over to the bed, putting the bag of my things that we'd brought from the hospital on top. I watch as he reaches for a box on the bed, and gasp when he tries to hand it to me.

"No," I tell him, shaking my head a little too much. "I can't accept that, D." It's a brand new iPhone. It costs way too much for me to possibly accept.

Fuck, everyone has already done way more for me than I want or deserve, but this is too far. I have enough money saved up to buy one of those shitty pay-as-you-go flip phones, and it will have to do.

"You can, and you will. We need to be able to get ahold of you when you're at school and not on the ranch," he says. The tone of his voice tells me I should just listen to him and take it, but I've never been someone to accept free shit. Especially when it's attached to pity.

"I only have one exam left before I graduate." I square my shoulders, looking him directly in the eye. "I would have already graduated if that night hadn't happened."

His eyebrows hit his hairline in surprise.

"Don't look so shocked, D," I mock, ignoring the pang or disappointment in my chest. Does he really think I'm incapable of graduating early?

"I just wasn't aware. Travis didn't tell me that after he talked to the school," he tells me. "We can call Principal Darvon and figure that all out if you'd like to do that later on. You can't be stressed out right now."

I sigh in annoyance, hating how everyone is treating me with kid gloves because of what happened. I've been through this song and dance before and came out of it just fine. I will do the same now.

I'll admit, the headache from the concussion has been much worse this time, and I'm still sensitive to light, but Doctor Evans thinks it's from having prior concussions. Still, the doctors ran the necessary tests to see if there was any damage in my brain before I even woke up, and they didn't find anything except some minor swelling.

I got lucky. But they did say to be exceptionally careful from here on out because anymore concussions could irrevocably damage my brain and eyesight. To say it scared me would be an understatement, but I don't want to be treated like some fragile glass, either. I won't break.

"The sooner I graduate, the sooner I can get a job and get out of your space," I tell him, my attitude shining through.

I'm so tired, but it's my only defence. I can't just let it go.

"You're not a burden, sweetness," he says gently, laying the phone back on the bed before resting his hands on my shoulders. "I know that piece of shit made you feel like you were less than, but you aren't." He looks at me with determination.

"D," I whisper. Between the emotions and exhaustion, I've lost what little energy I had when I woke up this morning.

"Get some sleep, Abbs. We can talk later." He removes his hands and points his finger directly at me. "And you're taking that phone. Rose already set it up, and there are probably a million messages."

I chuckle as he rolls his eyes, muttering something about women and their need to chat at all hours of the day. Moving to the bed and sitting down, I pick up the phone box when he walks to the door.

"Hey, D?" I call out, and he turns around. "Thanks. For everything."

His smile disarms me as he nods his head before leaving me alone to rest. Maybe, just maybe, this won't be so bad.

## CHAPTER 14
## DAMEON

As I leave Abigail to rest, my brain won't stop worrying about all of the what-ifs that can come from helping someone in her shoes to heal.

I've seen the effects that abuse can have on victims and women. I watched it happen to my own sister, for fuck's sake, but Lana was different. Her and Abigail are like night and day, and I'm certain their healing process won't be the same. It never really is.

Everyone heals differently, that much I know to be true. I wasn't talking out of my ass at the hospital when I laid it all out. I've done my research, and lived through my mom's episodes as well as Joe's. Everyone heals different from any given experience.

Hell, it took Lana four different therapists before she found one that could help her. Mind you, before

Travis' brother Derek, the others had a terrible habit of victim blaming.

Shaking my head, I bring myself back to the present and head into the kitchen. After taking stock of what I have in the fridge, I settle on one of my staples.

Grabbing what I need, I start laying it all out on the counters and get down to business. I may not be the best cook in the world, but I make do.

Normally, we all get together at the main house for dinner most nights, but we've also stocked our own cabins to make them fully functional for nights where we'd rather stay in. I know for a fact that Abby isn't ready to deal with that many people around her just yet, so I'm glad I made sure to have food in the fridge.

When Lana and Trent decided they were going to build their own cabin on the property for privacy, I chose to do the same. I don't have anything against my brothers, but Lana and I have always been different. We like our space, but more than that, we need it. I'm too hot headed to share a house with other people around the clock, and she feels too suffocated with all of us breathing down her neck all the time.

I've been living with people my entire life, but getting my own place without having to leave the ranch just felt right. I mean, I'm breaching on thirty here. It was time to spread my wings.

We're already building several smaller cabins anyway for anyone who comes to Serenity Stables for shelter and protection, so why not just build while contractors are already here? You know?

Joe has his own being built farther back on the property as well. I assume he will use it as more of a retreat spot than to actually live in it like I am, but who knows?

Setting the frying pan on the stove, I turn it to medium heat and add some oil to the bottom before tossing in the chopped onions I cut while lost in my thoughts.

I should probably pay more attention because don't even remember chopping it up, which is dangerous as fuck.

Once the onions are simmering and stirred, I lower the heat and prep the steaks, tossing them into the oven on this fancy-ass pan that my sister bought all of us for Christmas last year.

*"You need to eat healthier."* Is what she told us before explaining how to use the fucking things.

I'm not going to lie. Shit tastes almost as good as cooking it on a grill or over an open fire. Almost.

"What smells so good?" Abigail says behind me, almost scaring the living fuck out of me.

"Oh, uh..." I turn around to look at her, my heart rate picking up a bit when she smirks. I'd give anything to see her smile after she almost fucking died, but this is a close second.

"Wow, Dameon Easton is speechless? Call the press," she smarts off, and I roll my eyes.

"Not speechless, you just surprised me," I tell her. "Sometimes I forget I'm not alone when I have someone here."

It's the truth. There are times when Joe, Lana, and Carl have all snuck up on me. I'm pretty sure they make a game out of it, but it's not my fault I have a habit of zoning everything else out when I'm focused on a task in my own damn house.

She eyes me suspiciously for a moment. "That must get lonely."

Well, fuck. I wasn't expecting her to say that. If anyone knows a thing or two about being alone, it's probably her.

"It can be if I decide to stay cooped up too long," I say with a shrug. "Most of the time, though, I will just go to the main house or grab Lana and go for a ride with the horses."

"The horses," she says, perking up for the first

time in days. Maybe being out of the hospital is exactly what she needs.

"Can we go see them?" she asks then, and I smile.

"We can tomorrow. You can help us brush them down if you want," I tell her, enjoying the way she smiles wide at that. There it is.

Now I need to figure out how to keep that smile around. I don't want her to fall into a deep depressive state that leads her to cutting or self-harm if I can help it.

"Really?"

I chuckle. I forgot she hasn't really been around animals much. At least, not horses... but I've found a lot more people than you'd think actually love the idea of being near a horse, they just haven't experienced it.

"Yes, really. I have to wash Star down anyway," I tell her.

"Star?"

"She's my horse."

Her eyes widen in wonder and she reminds me of a little kid being told something exciting for the first time, before the light dims in her eyes and she looks away.

"Hey, what is it?" I ask.

I move around the counter to step in front of her,

careful not to get too close. Over the past week, I've learned that this look she gets is usually followed by some negative thoughts.

"What? Nothing, I'm fine," she lies, and I want nothing more than to remind her that lies aren't okay between us, but I can't.

Abigail doesn't know I like her, and for all intents and purposes, I fucking well can't like her that way, so I'm keeping my mouth shut.

For now. But I can probe a little to make sure she knows I'm looking out for her. When it comes to her health, both mental and physical, there definitely can't be secrets between us. She agreed to that before being discharged.

Unfortunately, whatever is going on in her head probably doesn't seem like the kind of thing she *needs* to tell me.

"Sweetness, come on. You know you can't keep things locked away because it leads to other actions." Actions I hate bringing up because I don't even want her to think about it.

The idea of her harming herself makes my heart ache. I know it's likely to happen again because it's a vicious cycle, but I hate it. She's been through enough.

She sighs, looking exhausted all of a sudden. "I feel stupid for getting so excited."

See? In her mind, she probably didn't think that pertained to her mental health enough to warrant mentioning.

"Why would that make you feel stupid? It's okay to get excited over things."

"I know." She shrugs, glancing back at me before looking out the kitchen window above the sink. "It's just not something I've been around much."

"What's not?" I ask, needing clarification. I want to know where her head is at.

"Everyone having their own horse, or even just a pet," she says quietly, and I nod in understanding.

"I don't think most places are equipped like ours. Unless you live on a ranch, most families don't have a horse for each person," I say. "Maybe one or two for the family that are held at a local stable, but not the setup we have."

She smiles softly as a tear runs down her cheek.

I move slowly to put my finger under her chin, gently moving her so she's looking me in the eye. "And not all families have pets, Abigail."

"I know. Told you it was silly."

"No," I tell her in a firm but gentle voice. "It's not

silly. You're friends with Rina. Do you know how excited she is to come here and ride with Lana?"

She sniffs but nods. "Yeah, she loves it here."

"She does, and I think you will too. Rina didn't grow up with animals either, but she's surrounded by them now. Whenever she wants." I grip her chin now, conveying how serious I am. "The same goes for you. Serenity is your home now, Abigail."

"Home, huh?" she breathes out, and I smile.

"Always."

# CHAPTER 15
# ABIGAIL

I DIDN'T THINK I WOULD STRUGGLE THIS MUCH ON MY first night out of the hospital.

Maybe it's all of the things reminding me of home and what Dad did that night, but it's eating me alive. I just want to scream and trash everything to find something, anything, to relieve this pressure building inside of me.

Dinner with Dameon was surprisingly nice. He treated me how I imagine he would treat anyone he had staying with them. He was kind and courteous, and didn't once look at me with an ounce of pity.

Hell, he even tried to help when the negative thoughts tried to weigh me down. Maybe that's what started all of this in the first place.

If I'm being honest, it's probably everything

compounded with the fact that I haven't felt that blade in a couple of weeks now, and it's hard. It's like I'm going through withdrawal.

Dr. Patrick warned me this would happen. How going cold turkey, while being the only real option with self-harm, is intense. I just didn't realize how intense it would truly be.

"Ugh!" I growl into the room, keeping my voice down so I don't draw attention to me. "Fuck it."

I grab the phone Dameon insisted I use, and dial Rose.

"Hey, babe!" she says cheerfully.

"How did you know it was me?" I ask, then groan. "He gave you this number the second he got it, didn't he?"

She laughs. "You bet. That man wasn't about to take no for an answer. Mind you, considering I set it up, I could have easily just stolen it."

Fair point. I also doubt anyone can say no to him. Any of the Easton men, really. They're kind of legendary in Haven Hills for being the strongest and some of the most intense people you'll ever meet.

"Thank you for helping pick out my books," I say quietly, my throat thick with emotion.

"Of course! If you're going to be laid up in bed

and recovering, you need those fictional hotties in your life!"

"You know, you could have grabbed my kindle and saved me the embarrassment," I scoff at her.

"First, there is nothing to be embarrassed about. You're allowed to like whatever you like. Second, I doubt your little books were even a second thought to him. You do know what they say around town, right?"

Yeah, I've heard all the rumours. Dameon Easton is a wild card. A bad boy with a heart of gold who also has a heavy hand when it comes to sex and play. A true sadist, apparently, and that's something I prefer to stay away from. I think I've been hit enough times in my life that personally signing up for something like that just doesn't sound appealing.

"You know how I feel about rumours," I remind her.

"I'm not spreading them, just giving you a mental reminder. If anything we've heard is true, then your kinky books won't phase him in the slightest."

Okay, she makes a good point, but I'd still like my kindle so I can read in the dark.

"But your kindle is there, babe. I put it in your underwear drawer."

I burst out laughing at the mere thought of her

sneaking about and sliding it into my personal shit. Did she think someone was going to rob the place, but leave my dresser untouched?

"Why the hell did you put it there?!" I can't stop laughing. It still hurts my ribs and stomach, but it lightens my soul, and right now I need as much light as I can get.

"Because! Some of the things you have on there belong in the drawer with your sexiest panties. By the way, you need to go to confession or something, babe. That shit is hot enough to land your ass in Hell."

"Oh my GOD! You didn't just say that!" I laugh even harder, groaning when it hurts too much.

"Eh, it got you to laugh." She's quiet for a moment. "How are you feeling?"

I close my eyes and take a deep breath to ground myself before responding. "Tired. Emotional."

"I think that's allowed given everything you've been through. But hey! You're turning eighteen in a few days! That's something to celebrate, right?!"

I don't really know how to feel about that. On the one hand, I'm so fucking excited to be able to do things without a parent or guardian, but on the other, it's a reminder that my carefully planned escape is no longer an option.

"It's... terrifying," I tell her truthfully.

"I know. Your entire plan has changed, but if you let it, this could be the best thing that's ever happened to you." She groans, making me smile. "Not the almost dying part or what you've had to live through. That shit is horrible and I hope your dad rots in prison as someone's soap bitch. I hope they beat the shit out of him at least once a week for sport to remind him of the pecking order, too. It's the least that bastard deserves!"

"Rose!" I gasp before choking on laughter.

"I said what I said, babe, and I make no apologies." She snickers. "But seriously, now you have something stable and solid. You can stay here for a while and be safe. Really come up with a plan before college."

She's right. Maybe this will be my chance at a new beginning. After all, Dameon said this was my home now too. Maybe I should stop being so pessimistic and focus on the positive narrative.

"You know what, Rosie? Maybe you're right."

"I hate you," she says with no heat. She really hates being called Rosie and says the only one allowed to do so is her grandfather.

"Bullshit. You love the fuck out of me." I smile into the room, settling back into the bed as the pressure eases inside of me just enough to get comfortable.

This weight? I can live with it. When everything starts to bubble over and I'm lost in my own mind with no distractions, that's when the demons like to play.

"I do love you. You're my best friend, which means it's my duty to tell you to go to sleep. You need the rest, babe."

"You're not kidding. I just wanted to say thank you for all of it."

I don't think I've ever said thank you to so many people in one day or ever felt this emotional all at once toward so many. It's kind of exhausting, but in a good way.

"You're welcome. Goodnight, babe."

"Night."

# CHAPTER 16
# DAMEON

LANA:

Star and Cocoa are ready whenever you are.

SHE'S REALLY EXCITED TO INTRODUCE ABIGAIL TO THE horses. Actually, she insisted on being there for the initial meet because they seemed to connect over how cute they find horses.

Cocoa is also Lana's horse, so if Abigail is going to eventually ride him, it's best that Lana does the introduction anyway.

"Hey, sleepyhead," I call out when the patter of footsteps echoes down the hallway.

"Ugh, rude," Abigail mumbles under her breath, and I snort, lifting my head to look at her.

The dark circles under her eyes are more prominent than they were yesterday, meaning she didn't sleep very well.

It's also pretty easy to tell that Abigail is not a morning person with how she greeted me, and it's fucking adorable.

"You okay?" I check in with her. I don't want her to feel pressured, but I need to make sure she's resting or her brain and body won't heal.

She winces, shaking some of the golden locks loose from her ponytail. Or what's left of one, anyway. It's hanging onto the side of her head for dear life, and I would almost bet there's more hair out of that ponytail than in it right now.

"I've never been much of a morning person." Her baby blues meet mine, and I can tell she's being honest. That's a good start to the day, so I won't push her on the sleep right now. She'll rest when she needs to, I'm sure.

"You mean you're not almost snarky and giving everyone a good ol' fuck you first thing in the morning?" I smirk so she knows I'm joking, and she laughs.

"Nah, you're just special, D," she sasses, easing my worry.

"Good to hear it." I nod, totally serious.

If she's going to give anyone shit, I rather it be me

than someone who can't take it. Besides, I think there's more to her ribbing me, the same way there's this unnerving need inside of me to make sure she takes care of herself.

She would have been perfectly healthy and safe with Travis and Rina, but I needed her here where I could keep an eye on her personally.

"Don't you have to go to work?" she asks, changing the subject through a yawn.

"No. At least, not yet. I'm going to the barn to brush the horses down and clean their stalls." Her face starts to shut down, but I don't stop talking. "You're welcome to come with me and help. Lana will be there with Cocoa," I finish, and her entire face lights up.

"Seriously?!" I nod. "Yes! Please, yes! Okay, I need to go get changed." She starts running toward the bedrooms, all evidence of exhaustion gone for the time being.

"Breakfast first, then get ready." I make sure to use my no nonsense tone of voice that has most people listening without question.

"Not hungry!" she calls back, still moving.

"Abigail." This time I use my Dom voice, and she stops in her tracks.

Good, that'll come in handy later. Knowing

Abby, she's going to test me more than anyone else ever has.

"Yeah?" she asks, turning around slowly to look at me.

God, she's beautiful like this. Happy and flushed from excitement. If seeing the horses keeps that smile on her face, I'll make sure she gets a chance to spend time with them every day. Especially when her being happy will help her mental health.

"You need to eat," I tell her slowly, crossing my arms over my chest.

"But—"

"Food, Abby."

"I wasn't lying when I said I'm not hungry. I don't really eat breakfast." Her eyes turn away from me at the end.

"Your body needs the nutrients to heal. We talked about this, remember?" I ask quietly, walking over to stand in front of her.

"Eating things in the morning makes me queasy," she admits softly, and I frown.

"You ate breakfast at the hospital."

"And I had to force myself to lay still for at least an hour afterward," she glances at me with a guilty look in her eyes.

"Why didn't you tell someone sooner?"

She shrugs, before straightening her shoulders and back as though she's preparing for a fight. I fucking hate it. "Like you said, I need to eat in order to heal."

Taking her chin in my hand, I raise her eyes to meet mine. "There are alternatives to actual food. Have you tried smoothies in the mornings?"

I truly want to help her work through this so that she's healthy, and I remember Mom used to make us smoothies when we were sick. They were just all around easier to get down and stomach.

"Not in years. Mom——" she chokes out. "Mom used to make them for us a couple times a week."

Oh, sweetness. Fuck me. All I want to do is pull her into a hug right now, but I know Abby will take it as a form of pity, and it would just make her angry.

"Yeah? How about we make a deal?" I raise my eyebrow in question, and she eyes me warily.

"What sort of deal?" she questions, staring me down.

I chuckle, giving her chin a small squeeze before pulling my hand back. "You can get dressed——"

"YES!"

"BUT, we go to the main house for a smoothie before we head to the barn."

"Buzzkill," she grumbles, but the curve of her

lips betrays her. "Alright, I'll try it. Maybe it won't be so bad. Just don't put something weird in it like kale or some crap." She gags, making me chuckle.

"Hmm, that's a tough sell. I hear Kale has a lot of great nutrients in it." She narrows her eyes at me. "Fine. For today, I promise there will be no kale in your smoothie."

"Never kale."

"We'll see, sweetness. I'm sure there's a way to mask the flavour of it somehow."

She snorts, backing away. "The day I see you drink a smoothie with kale in it, Dameon Easton, is the day I will try it."

Fuck.

The face I make must portray my thoughts because she burst into giggles as she turns away and heads down the hall to her room.

Now I have to decide. Is kale really that important for her to have in her smoothies?

Unfortunately, I already know the answer to that question without having to look it up.

Guess I'm looking for recipes to mask the taste of that god-awful shit because a deal is a deal. And her being healthy trumps my displeasure for the gross green crap.

## CHAPTER 17
## ABIGAIL

WHEN WE WALK INTO THE BARN AFTER GOING TO THE main house, Lana is beaming from ear to ear. She runs up to me and pulls me into a giant hug, almost knocking the shake out of my hand.

"Easy, firecracker," D says in a scolding tone. "You're going to knock her breakfast out of her hands."

Gee, what a shame that would be.

Actually, all things considered, it's pretty tasty. He added strawberries and bananas with some Greek yogurt and almond milk. The only thing I don't love about it is the spinach, but given a choice between that or kale, I will choose spinach every time.

"Oh!" Lana squeaks, jumping away from me like I burned her. "Sorry."

I glare at D as I shake my head. "Don't be. He's just trying to be a tyrant and worried that I'll refuse to eat if this one ends up on the ground." I smile sweetly at Lana.

"Ooo, you got a smoothie for breakfast?" she asks, looking at her brother in awe. "I want a smoothie."

"Are you sure? He insists on putting spinach in it," I tell her, gagging when I take a drink just to drive D a little insane.

She giggles, and it's honestly adorable how carefree she seems. After what she went through with her ex, it's almost a miracle she's able to be so happy. But Rina is the same way, too. They've both been through tragic darkness and still manage to find happiness in the world. I can only hope that one day I'll be able to do the same.

"You did have breakfast today, right?" Dameon asks her, crossing his arms over his chest and ignoring my attempt to get a rise out of him.

"Obviously," she says with sass, making me laugh. I think her and I are going to be great friends.

"Oh yeah? What did you eat?" Clearly he doesn't

believe her. Glad it's not just me that he's suspicious of, I focus on Lana and wait for her response.

She rolls her eyes at him, and I see his jaw tick from the corner of my eye. "Food." She crosses her arms over her chest and lifts her chin in clear defiance.

Watching these two go toe-to-toe is the most fun I've had in weeks. Wow, that's kind of depressing, actually.

"Try again, little sis," Dameon says, and Lana's eyes flare at the clear power pull he's trying to make.

"What I had for breakfast doesn't matter," she says, refusing to back down.

It's pretty clear she's trying to distract him with her defiance so he won't realize she probably hasn't eaten anything, but I think we all know he isn't falling for it.

Props to her for trying though.

"What are you doing?" she asks, dropping her arms and stepping toward him, but he moves back.

"You know exactly what I'm doing," he replies, lifting his cell to his ear.

"Oh crapadoodle!" she false curses and stomps her foot.

"Trent. Hey, man," D says into the phone, and my

eyes grow wide. He called her fiancé? Holy shit! What kind of brother betrayal move is that? Sheesh.

"I should have seen this coming," Lana mumbles at the same time her stomach growls loud enough to have D and I both quirking a brow. "Traitor," she growls down at stomach.

"Want my smoothie?" I ask her happily, ready to hand it over to her. It's not like I actually need it this morning.

"Don't even think about it, sweetness," Dameon growls out, hanging up the phone.

"She's hungry and I'm not. Besides, you seem to be having a coronary over her not eating, so really, I'm just being helpful," I smart off.

Lana chokes on a laugh, and I smirk. I feel oddly proud that I'm able to be a pain in the ass. It's the most I've felt like myself in weeks, too. It's great.

"Being helpful, you say?" he asks, his voice dropping low.

Fuck, that tone does things to my traitorous body. *Having the hots for Dameon Easton is not an option, body, chill.*

"You bet!" I reply, moving toward Lana with the cup held out.

Her eyes travel between D and I before she

shakes her head no, and I sigh. Damn, it was worth a shot.

"Why are you all up her ass over eating breakfast anyway?" I change tactics, throwing him off. "She's here to help us. You should really be nicer to her."

"Nicer to her." His words are an echo of my own.

"Yes, nicer. I know it's a foreign concept to a sourpuss such as yourself, but really, dude." If I thought the twitch of his jaw was intense when Lana was avoiding his question, it's way worse now.

Whoops.

"Sourpuss." He repeats my words again, and I frown at him, feigning concern.

"Are you broken?" I question, tilting my head to assess him.

Lana bursts into laughter beside us, loving the banter we've got going on. I have to admit, it's quite fun. I'm definitely enjoying myself.

"Oh man," Lana says between gasps of laughter. "You are in so much trouble."

"Yes, firecracker, she is." Dameon turns to her. "But so are you. Lying?"

She sobers up fast, and I almost want to slap him on the back of the head.

"I was just so excited to come out here!" she

pleads with him, and his eyes soften as he takes her in.

"I'm glad you're excited, and I'm glad you're here to help us," he says, moving over to her and ignoring me for time time being. I take the opportunity to chug down the rest of the shake, hoping it stays down without making me ill.

"I really am sorry," she says gently, and he sighs.

"I know you are, but you need to eat just as much as Abby does," he tells her, and she groans.

"I promise I'll eat when we're finished."

"Oh, I know you will. Trent is on his way home with some breakfast."

"Crap," she grumbles, making him laugh.

"He sounds overly intent on making sure you don't do this again."

"Of course he does," she grumbles. "We better get this meet-and-greet out of the way before he gets here, then."

Dameon holds his arm out, and I watch as she curls into his side, hugging his waist. "You know it's because we love you," he tells her.

"I know, I know. I just get really excited sometimes."

He smiles down at her. "I know you do. Trent

assured me you could come back out to see Cocoa after you eat and have a chat."

"Sure, a chat." Lana snorts, pulling away from him. "I'll go over there and wait for you." She stands on her toes and kisses D's cheek before winking at me as she walks past.

"I'm confused," I admit. I don't really know what she meant with that snort, and my curiosity is getting the better of me.

"What are you confused on?" he asks, smirking at me. "Lana's attitude?"

"No, that part I get." I smirk at him. "I love women with attitude."

"Oh, I just bet you do, sweetness." He takes a step closer to me. "You seem happier."

I shrug with a smile. "I feel happier."

"Good," he whispers, taking one more step and leaning down to whisper into my ear. "I love seeing that fire in your eyes, sweetness. Don't ever lose it again."

He pulls away and holds out a hand, waving me in the direction Lana went, and I gladly turn and head toward her. Anything to make sure the affect he has on me stays hidden.

## CHAPTER 18
## DAMEON

SEEING THE FIRE COME BACK TO ABIGAIL A FEW minutes ago was worth the headache I now have from grinding my teeth. Between Lana lying to me and starting with the sass, then Abigail jumping in to try and save her, it took all of my will to not respond.

I'm used to my sister being forgetful and trying to fool us when we realize she hasn't eaten. If it has to do with her spending time with her horse, Cocoa, she has a one track mind. As much as her forgetting to eat is frustrating, it's the lying that set me off.

Something is going on with her. That's why I called Trent and why he's coming home. We both think she's just trying to do too much and not resting enough.

"Oh my," Abby gasps, drawing my attention to her.

She's staring at Cocoa and Star like they're the most beautiful animals she has ever seen.

"They're beautiful, aren't they?" Lana says reverently, snuggling close to her horse's snout and breathing deeply.

Yeah, something is really bothering her.

"Gorgeous," Abby says, choking on a sob. "Can I pet him?"

"Of course!" Lana replies, holding her hand out to Abby. "Cocoa, this is Abby. She's super sweet and needs lots of loving, so be nice." She's pretending to scold the horse, but he's more than used to my sister's antics by now.

He moves his nose to nuzzle Lana's cheek, making her giggle, then turns his attention to Abby. He watches her, waiting for her to make the first move.

"Hold your hand out so he can smell you, Abbs," I tell her gently, walking up behind them.

"Oh." She moves her hand before her, holding her breath as Cocoa starts to sniff. "His nose is so soft," she whispers in awe, and I smile.

"Yeah, it's one of the things I love about horses." I squeeze her shoulders in support.

"Me too. They give the best nuzzles," Lana says, sighing in contentment. She moves to hide her face in Cocoa's neck, like she's hiding from the world.

While Abby is paying attention to Cocoa and petting his nose, I pull my phone out to send Trent a message.

ME:

> Something is wrong, man. Lana is holding onto Cocoa for dear life. I don't think this has anything to do with being bratty.

TRENT:

> Fuck. Thanks, Dameon. I'll talk to her. I'm just leaving the store. Be home soon.

Pocketing the phone, I focus my attention on the girls, and notice how close they've huddled together to whisper.

"Anyone want to share the secrets of the universe with me?" I ask, knowing it will lighten the mood.

"Why would we do that, D? That seems like a terrible idea," Abby snarks, making Lana giggle.

I'll allow it to make my sister happy, but is she

thinks I'm going to forget the comments she made this morning, she has another think coming. I may not be her dominant, but I am her guardian for the time being. That means setting some boundaries and knowing how far is too far.

"I don't know." I shrug with a smirk. "You two just seem like you're sharing top secrets with the way you're canoodling over there. And Cocoa is an accomplice."

"He is not!" Lana gasps, warming my heart. Perfect, she's going into little space just enough to relax a bit without being overly noticeable to Abigail.

"Hmm, I don't know," I murmur, eyeing the horse in question. "What do you think, Star? Is your boyfriend an accomplice?" I ask my horse, really playing it up now just for the fun of it.

Star stares at me like she's bored, but moves her head to nuzzle me anyway.

"Star would never betray Cocoa," Lana says with a smirk. "Didn't you know that husbands and wives can't speak against one another's alleged crimes in a court of law?" she asks me.

"And that's enough crime tv for you, sweet pea," Trent says from the barn door, shaking his head.

Lana squeals and runs toward him, jumping in

his arms so fast she almost knocks him over. "Daddy!"

The second she starts crying, a look of true worry comes to rest on Trent's face. Abby and I watch him wrap his arms around her and carry her out of the barn with a quick nod toward us.

"Is she okay?" Abby asks when they're both gone, leaning her cheek onto the top of Cocoa's nose. I love the fact that she's already drawn to the horses for comfort after just a few minutes.

"Honestly? I don't know, but I don't think so," I tell her the truth. If we're going to build a foundation of trust, I have to be just as open with her as she needs to be with me.

"What do you think it is?" She sounds worried as she looks toward the door where they left.

"Trent thought it was exams a couple of weeks ago, but those are finished now. I honestly can't tell you." I shake my head. "He'll figure it out though. He always does."

Abigail scrunches her nose in thought before looking directly at me. "You're worried about her." It's a statement not a question.

"I'm always worried about her. She's my little sister and she's been through a lot. But she's in good hands with Trent. I know she'll be okay." The truth of those words saddens me a little.

Lana and I were thick as thieves as kids, and while that won't ever change, it has shifted. I'm not the first one she runs to anymore when she needs help.

"I'm sorry you have to add me to your stressors," Abby says quietly.

"No. You are a lot of things, sweetness, but a stressor is not one of them. You hear me?"

She's quiet for a moment before giving me a curt nod, then looks around the barn. "So, are we going to brush the horses or what?"

"Yeah. Well, I'll show you how to brush them and then move to mucking the stalls."

I don't miss the adorable look of disgust that crosses her face. Not that she finds horses gross—probably, anyway—but the idea of shovelling shit is definitely not sitting well with her stomach.

"Sounds like a plan." Her hand moves to her stomach.

"Feeling sick?" She chugged that shake pretty fast, so it could be coming back on her.

"Kind of? Not really, though. I just feel nervous, I think."

"Nothing to be nervous about, but if that changes, let me know."

"Promise." She makes an x over her heart with her finger before holding up her hand. "Can I brush them now? Please?"

"Sure," I say with a laugh. I'm not sure I could deny her anything after that adorable act.

## CHAPTER 19
## ABIGAIL

"Can we do that again tomorrow?" I ask Dameon after we've cleaned up from dinner.

He chuckles, sitting down on the couch beside me. "Sure, Abbs. We can hang out with the horses as much as you want."

I clap my hands in excitement before staring down at them in wonder. When was the last time I felt excited about something?

Hell, when was the last time I felt like I could breathe as easily as I do now?

"Where did you go just now?" he asks me, drawing my focus back to him.

"Honestly?"

"Always," he reminds me, and I nod.

"I was trying to remember the last time I was

ever excited for something," I admit, moving my eyes from his.

"We'll just have to make sure you're excited for a lot of things then, won't we?"

I frown. "You can't just change everything, Dameon. It's not that simple."

He sighs, running his hand down his face. He looks tired.

"I appreciate you wanting to, but some things are just the way they are," I explain. Suddenly I feel like I'm not explaining myself right.

After a moment of thought, I shuffle closer to him, bringing my knee up and turning my body so we're face to face.

"What are you doing, sweetness?" he asks in confusion.

"I'm having a hard time explaining what I mean." I shake my head. "It's kind of coming out all wrong and I feel like an ass."

"You're not an ass, sweetness. Don't say negative shit about yourself."

"Again, I appreciate that, but I'm just saying I feel like I'm coming across as one. Not that I am one," I explain slowly. "I am so grateful for everything you've done for me these past two weeks. You saved my life, D. I'm just saying... making everything exciting is unrealistic. It's not real life, and I'm better off knowing that."

"What?" He moves even closer. "There is so much in life to be excited about, Abigail. Just because you're able to find excitement in things again, doesn't mean it will all come crashing down."

The second my worst fear is put into words, I feel my chest constrict with anxiety. That's really what my apprehension is about. I'm so worried that I'll crash hard when I leave here, and the sadness and depression I felt before will multiply to a point where I'm unable to handle it.

I don't want to get my hopes up.

"I love that you want me to be excited over things, but I'm telling you to not get your hopes up. I've been this way for too long to believe it will change overnight," I snap out, choosing anger over panic because it's a lot easier to lean into.

He narrows his eyes at me, moving to cup my face in his hands and forcing me to look at him. "I'm not saying anything is going to happen overnight, but I'm going to be with you every step of the way, Abigail Davies. We all will." The conviction in his voice is terrifying to me because I know he truly believes that.

"D," I whisper, and he shakes his head.

"Nope. You don't get to give up on day one, Abigail. You need to at least try and have faith."

Tears start pooling in my eyes as I look at him. How the hell did we get here? The man everyone in town talks about being a controlling sadist, loving to dole out pain to willing women, and the girl that feels the need to run away from everything she knows? It's like a bad plot for a television show. I just can't decide whether it'd be a sitcom or horror.

"I'm scared," I whisper my truth. I promised him and Dr. Patrick that I would be honest no matter what. This is me keeping that promise.

"I know." He lets out a harsh breath. "It's normal to be scared, but please, Abbs. Don't give up. Ever." He moves closer to me so our noses are almost touching, and my breath hitches.

He's not going to kiss me, right? That wouldn't be wise. It would also be illegal. I think.

*Then why is your heart beating faster at the thought of him kissing you?*

Dameon's eyes darken as they scan mine before he squeezes my face once more. "Never fucking stop fighting, sweetness," he growls before pulling away.

I swallow, feeling cold without him close. "I'll do the best I can," I promise him, standing with him when he gets up. "I just can't promise it will be a smooth process."

"Nothing good in life is easy, Abbs, but it is worth it." When I try to answer, I yawn before words can come out, and he chuckles. "Get some sleep. You've had a long day and you're still recovering."

He's not wrong. I'm so fucking tired now that I've had a chance to sit down. I really should have taken a nap earlier, but I couldn't tear myself away from Cocoa and Star.

"The fact that I'm exhausted at eight pm is just depressing," I grumble, making him laugh.

"Welcome to living on a ranch, Abbs. Get used to it."

Yeah, right. There's no way I'll feel like this after I completely heal.

"Doubtful. I'm not old like you, D," I pop off, taking a few steps backward.

"There's that damn sass again," he groans. "We'll be talking about that tomorrow. Be careful with that mouth of yours, Abigail. I may just have to teach it a lesson."

With that, D walks away, leaving me gaping at him and feeling flushed all over. He did not just say that to me. And he definitely didn't mean what I'm envisioning...right?

The closing of his door snaps me out of my stupor. Shutting the lights off, I use the flashlight on my phone to go to the bathroom before heading to bed.

By the time I've changed into pjs and crawled under the cool blankets, my mind is still conjuring up the dirtiest of fantasies. Ones with the youngest Easton brother using his cock to teach my mouth a lesson.

For shits and giggles, I decide to double check the age of consent for Nebraska, and almost drop my phone on my face. Sixteen? Well, that's convenient, now isn't it?

*Fuck. I really need to get my hormones under control. This is ridiculous. Maybe I need to find a way to hook up with Ted and work some of this tension out.*

# CHAPTER 20
# DAMEON

WHAT THE FUCK IS WRONG WITH ME?! ABIGAIL IS probably in her room right now, thinking I've threatened to fuck her mouth when all I meant was I'd wash it out with soap. Fucking hell, I'm in deep shit here.

I would never insinuate something sexual with her while she's this vulnerable, and sure as fuck not when I know there's a great chance she can't handle the darker side of me.

It's bad enough I almost kissed her tonight. The moment her breath caught, I wanted to give in and taste that pouty goddamn mouth that gives me so much grief on the daily. But I couldn't, and I won't. Just because she seems like she wants it, wants me, doesn't mean I can make a move on her.

There is so much going on with Abigail's mental health and her life right now, it would make me the shittiest of assholes if I took advantage of that. Maybe there are some guys out there willing to do something so low, but I am not one of them.

Tomorrow is a new day, and hopefully with that, a positive outlook on life again because we have some things we really need to discuss.

"Someone looks grumpy this morning," Abigail teases.

We're in the main house so I can make her another shake, and it seems my words didn't upset her last night because she's sassier than ever.

"I'm not grumpy, smartass, I'm tired. There is a difference," I tell her, turning the blender on.

"Tomato, to-ma-toh," she snarks once I've shut the blender off.

"Yeah, yeah."

"D," she says, her voice turning serious. "Did I do something wrong?"

Fuck. "No, Abbs, you didn't." I wince. "But only because we never talked about ground rules like we should have when you moved in."

"Rules. Seriously, D? Tomorrow is my birthday. I'm basically eighteen. I don't need rules."

I can't help but snort at that comment. If she thinks her being eighteen is going to mean she doesn't need rules, she has another think coming because she definitely needs them. As much for structure and support as to teach her how and when she should use discretion with that sassy mouth of hers.

"Being eighteen doesn't automatically make you know everything, sweetness," I tell her gently.

"I know that." She frowns. "Okay, what are these rules?"

I hate how she sinks in on herself like she's preparing for a lashing. Actually, it fucking infuriates me.

"Don't do that, Abbs. Don't curl in on yourself. I promise I will never hurt you." *Not without you asking me to, anyway.*

Shit. Someone needs to deck me in the face as hard as they can. Maybe it'll knock some goddamn sense into me.

"I—I know," she whispers, then straightens herself up. It's that inner strength that has made her the survivor she is. "I can't change how I react sometimes."

"I get that. It just makes me so fucking angry to see you like that. It makes me want to waltz into that jail and beat the fuck out of your father until he's no longer breathing," I seethe, and she blinks at me before smirking.

"Thanks, D. If it makes you feel any better, Rose says she hopes he becomes someone's soap bitch, and that they take turns beating him every week to remind him that he's a piece of shit."

"Rose?" I question, barking out a laugh. "The same girl I met that looks more like she belongs in a royal palace rather than here in Haven Hills?"

Abigail nods, joining me in my laughter, and the tension leaves her. "One and the same."

"Damn, that's cold. I fucking love it." I slap the table happily. "I'm on board with that plan."

"You're both crazy, but I appreciate it." Abigail takes a deep breath and levels me with a look. "Alright, then. Down to business. What are these rules?"

"Right." Taking a seat across from her at table, I get straight to the point. "You already know I'm going to make sure you're eating and well rested."

"Yep. I think you've made me eat more than I have in I don't even know how long. I'm beyond stuffed."

"Good. Let's keep it that way. Second, safety. I need you to be safe at all times." When she doesn't say anything, I elaborate, needing to get this point across. "For the time being, I don't want you going anywhere alone. If you absolutely have to, you're to tell me where you're going and when you'll be back. As well as with whom."

"Hell, no. That's ridiculous!" Abigail snarls, completely furious. "I'm not a child, Dameon. Don't you fucking dare treat me like one!"

"I'm not. Lana has the same rules as well. This isn't about control, Abigail. It's about safety," I explain.

"Lana has the same rules? Seriously?"

"She does. While Serenity may be the safest place around here and impossible to break into, there's still a lot of bad shit out there."

"I don't need a reminder of the bad shit in this world. I live with it every day." Her jaw tenses like she's bracing for a fight, and I find myself needing to be clear.

"Lana was almost killed by her ex. Then he talked her into sneaking out in the middle of the night and almost ran away with her. He beat her again before we found them." I take a calming breath to steady myself. "Rina's ex and father tried to kill her. They set fire to a barn and fucked with everyone's trucks so she was left alone with Lana before he kidnapped them both."

"Shit," she whispers.

"He beat Rina within an inch of her life, and would have killed her if Lana hadn't been there. Do you see why safety is so important now?" I ask her, my voice pleading with her to understand why I don't want her to be alone.

"I'm sorry. I never—I didn't think about things like that," she sighed. "I didn't know the full details, but yeah, I get it."

"And you agree to the rules so we can all keep you safe?"

"Definitely. Just promise me I won't be a prisoner. I have a life, D," she says quietly, and I nod.

"You're not a prisoner. We just want to keep you safe." I'll be finding a way to add a tracker on her, though.

Abby may be the one person in this town more hotheaded than I am. I know from personal experience how that type of behaviour can lead you down a defiant path, uncaring of the outcome. I already have a tracker on her phone, but if she ever did find it or run, I'm not sure she would take it with her.

"Okay, good. Any other rules?" She finishes off her smoothie and pushes the glass to the side.

"Just one for now," I start. "I'm glad you're finding your fire again, Abigail, so don't get me wrong when I say this. But you need to learn what lines not to cross when you're sassing me."

When her eyes widen and she takes a sharp breath, I know she's figured out what lines she crossed yesterday.

"I was just trying to help Lana," she states, but I shake my head.

"You didn't need to ask me why I was all 'up in her business'. Especially not in the crass way you chose to."

"I'm not used to being around people that care. It felt like you were attacking her, so I got defensive."

Fucking hell. She felt like I was attacking my sister because I was worried about her?

The reality that, outside of Rose, no one has shown Abigail any form of true caring and love since her mother died pains me. She deserves so much goddamn love she's practically smothered by it, and I will make sure we give it to her.

Whether she's ready for it or not, we're making Abigail a part of this family. For good.

"I would never hurt my sister or any other

woman, Abbs. You need to know that about me right now."

Something flashes in her eyes, but it's gone before I can fully catch it. If I had to guess, she's probably heard some of the rumours about me floating around town.

Unfortunately, unless you're in the kink lifestyle, those types of rumours are usually misconstrued into violence when it's not. But that's a conversation we will have if she ever brings it up.

"You're a good man, D," she tells me instead of asking the question on the tip of her tongue.

"Thank you. I sure as fuck try to be the best person I can be." Standing up, I smile at her. "Come on, sweetness. Let's go see the horses."

"YES!" she squeals and jumps to her feet, doing a little dance. She's so fucking cute when she lets herself feel excitement.

As we make our way toward the barn, a small part of my mind is telling me to question why I'm feeling a pull to more cute and adorable things over the sexy shit I've always been in to. But the rest of me just can't seem to find it in me to care.

I'm enjoying taking care of Abigail and making her smile, and right now, that's all that matters.

# CHAPTER 21
## ABIGAIL

"AH!!!!" Throwing my textbook across the room, I get off the bed and start pacing.

*Turn eighteen and everything will be okay.*

That's what I have told myself dozens of times a day for years. But it's not as simple as that anymore.

It's no longer about me just leaving my father and this town behind. It's about surviving the trauma he's caused me, and that can only be done here. At least, this is the one place I feel safe, and I'm just not ready to give that up yet.

"Abigail!" D slams through the door, almost knocking it from the hinges.

"What the fuck?!" I'm screeching as my heart races. "You scared the life out of me, asshole!"

"Me?" he asks, looking baffled. "You screamed

and there was a thud. I thought something happened to you!"

I scoff. "Sure. My final exam happened."

"What?"

Aww, he's confused. It's kind of adorable. Or it would be if I wasn't so frustrated and ready to have a mental breakdown. I'm verging on the edge of panic, and it's going to make me spiral.

I can't study for the exam when focusing so hard is giving me a migraine, and I'm sure as fuck not about to take an exam when I can't study beforehand.

"You know, I told myself that as soon as I turned eighteen, I'd be free. No more school, no more dealing with my father." I shake my head and flop onto the bed, feeling exhausted.

"Okay," he hedges, moving to sit at the foot of my bed. "What does that have to do with what's going on right now?"

"I turned eighteen three days ago, Dameon. You know what I have to show for it?" I ask him tiredly.

"A relatively kick-ass, low-key party?" he teases, making me roll my eyes.

It may have just been a small get together here at the stables with the Eastons and Rose, but it was the best birthday I've had in a long time, so yeah. It was pretty great.

"No, smartass, an email."

"An email," he states. "Abbs, you're going to have to work with me here, sweetness. I'm not following."

Of course he's not. I'm barely making any sense to myself right now, I'm so damn tired.

"I received an email yesterday from the school's new guidance counsellor, informing me that I have yet to finish my exams on time in order to graduate on my preferred timeline," I tell D as I reach for the ibuprofen on my nightstand.

"Excuse me?" he says. His voice is cold and I pause with the glass of water halfway to my mouth.

"Uh..." My words are muffled by the pills on my tongue, but I don't exactly know what I said wrong so I'm a bit confused at the anger radiating from him.

"Swallow the meds then talk," he orders, and I do as he says. I hate the taste of these damn things. So gross.

"Okay," I start, setting the glass back on my stand. "Why are *you* angry?" I know why I'm angry, but what does he have to be so mad about?

"You're recovering from a severe concussion, Abigail. There is no reason that they should have attempted to even send you a message this soon," he growls.

"Tell me about it." Yeah, I should probably know better than to smart off to him, but truthfully, this whole thing sucks.

"You need to go to sleep and get some rest. Worry about graduating when you're fully recovered, Abbs."

Easy for him to say. But he's right. At least for tonight, I have to call it, but I will start back into it first thing in the morning, migraine or not.

"Your head hurts?" D asks me once I've maneuvered myself under the covers. I was already in my pjs before I cracked the textbook open, thankfully, because my head is starting to throb way too much to move off the bed now. I would definitely be sleeping in my day clothes otherwise.

"So much," I whimper before I can stop myself.

"No phone, no lights, nothing, Abigail. I want you to get some sleep. If it's still bad in the morning, we'll call Richard."

I groan at his sternness and bring the blanket up over my head. "No. No doctor."

I get that he's worried about me, but he can't truly understand how much weight will be lifted from my shoulders when I have that diploma in my hand. If that means I have to fight through a few migraines, I will, because I never want to be in a situation where I feel like I've failed myself, and that's currently what's eating away at me.

Logical or not, it won't let up.

"Remember the rules? When it comes to your health and safety, I'm in charge. Terrible migraines after a concussion fall under that category," he reminds me.

I hear the click of my light switch before he comes back to the bed and pulls my blanket away from my face.

"Noooo. My bankie."

If I were more with it, I'd be seriously wondering where the hell that came from, but right now, I don't care. I just want my blanket and to sleep.

"You're going to suffocate yourself. Keep it off your head," he demands as he tucks me in so tight I can barely breathe.

"Dude," I whine and wiggle to loosen the burrito he's tried to put me in. "I still need to breathe."

Dameon huffs out a laugh, making me smirk. I can't see him since my eyes are closed, but I bet he's trying to decide if he finds my sass cute or annoying right now.

It's a fifty-fifty toss up, really. I've noticed that the

majority of the time, even when it does annoy him, he still finds it amusing which makes me feel better. It's a part of who I am and it's definitely not going anywhere, and living with someone who can't stand your personality? Definitely not something I ever want to experience again.

"Get some sleep, sweetness."

"Night, D."

"Goodnight. Sleep well."

"Okee," I say through a yawn before snuggling deep into the bed and falling asleep so quickly, I don't hear him leave.

## CHAPTER 22
## DAMEON

I HATE THAT I HAD TO LEAVE HER TODAY.

She's been pushing herself a lot the past couple of days, trying to study through migraines, and no matter what I do or say, she sneaks the damn books anyway.

If Abigail were mine, I would be spanking her ass so damn good she couldn't sit for a fucking month. She's putting herself in danger, and I'm at a loss. Which leads me to leaving her with Lana today.

When I called Richard and told him what was going on, he asked me to bring her in, but she refuses to see a doctor. And since she is now eighteen, we can't actually force her to see one. But that doesn't mean I can't seek out help on my own. If I can find anything to help her, I will.

"Dr. Evans will see you now, dear," Mrs. Smith greets me warmly.

Honestly, I'm beginning to think Lana is right and she's immortal or something. I swear, the old lady has been working here longer than we've been alive, and she shows no signs of slowing down yet.

Hell, I hope to have that kind of energy when I hit my eighties.

"Thank you, Mrs. Smith." I smile at her and head back to Richard's office, knocking once I reach the door.

"Come in," he calls. "Dameon," he greets as I close the door and take a seat.

"Hey, Doc."

"How was Abigail doing this morning?" he asks, focusing all of his attention on me. It's nice to see that some doctors actually still care about their patients because that's becoming harder and harder to find nowadays.

"Honestly? I don't know, man. She's pushing herself way too hard and I'm worried she's going to cause more damage than it's worth."

He sighs, leaning back in his chair. "I understand where you're coming from, and you have every right to be concerned. She needs to pace herself. This isn't a quick recovery."

I nod. "But she's not. She's trying to cram for hours at a time and the migraines seem to be getting worse."

"Has she gotten sick at all?" he questions after a moment.

"I don't think so? I haven't heard her anyway, and she definitely hasn't told me anything if she has. You think that's a possibility?"

"It could be, and if she does start throwing up, then she needs to be seen again immediately. She will need to have a scan done to make sure she's not making the swelling worse." He looks as worried as I feel as he explains the ramifications of what Abby may be doing to herself.

"Hopefully we don't get to that point." I sigh. "In the meantime, what can I do?"

"Here," he says, passing me a folder of papers. "It's generic stuff, really, but it may help." I take and open the folder, skimming through everything as he continues. "Try and get her to take a break every hour or so to give her eyes and head a rest. Remind her that smaller, more frequent sessions will go a long way right now. That she will be able to retain more information if her mind can rest in between."

"That should help the migraines as well, yes?" I ask, closing the folder.

"It should, yes. I would also try and keep the lights in the house dimmer if that's possible. Lower light is more relaxing and could help ease the pain as well. And lots of water. You have to make sure she's hydrated and getting as much rest as she can," he states as my phone rings.

"Sorry, that's Lana. I have to get this. She's staying with Abby right now," I tell him, taking my phone out and answering it. "Hey, firecrack—"

"You need to come home," she cries, frantic, and I jump to my feet.

"What's going on, Lana? Talk to me." I wave at Richard while heading out the door. He mimes for me to call him, and I nod and run to the truck as I listen to my sister panic.

"I don't know!" she wails, sounding like she's panicking. "She was in the bedroom. She said she needed to lie down, so I didn't bother her."

"Okay, slow down, firecracker. Breathe for me, okay?" I guide as I jump back in the truck and head straight for the ranch. "Good job, now continue. What happened?"

I'm trying my damnedest not to growl at my little sister because whatever happened sure as fuck isn't her fault, but I hate the sound of panic in her voice. My thoughts are racing about everything that could have gone wrong while I was away.

"She... I heard things breaking and when I tried to get into the bedroom, the door was locked. I can't get in, Dameon, and she won't talk to me. She just says to go away, but I'm so scared."

Fuck. If Abigail has locked everyone out and destroyed her room, I have a pretty good idea of what's happening behind that door. I don't like it, but I knew there was a strong possibility of it happening again. You don't just get past self-harming because you want to. It's a coping mechanism, and in many ways can be seen the same as substance addiction.

The temporary euphoria cutters feel when they see the blood flowing is almost like a high for them, and this exam shit has pushed Abigail too far. She's put too much stress on herself and cracked.

"Hey, it'll be alright. I'm on my way back now and will be there soon. Can you call Trent to come sit with you until then?" I ask, needing to soothe her. She's my priority as much as the woman that's locked herself away from the world.

"H-he's here now," she whimpers, and Trent takes the phone.

"I'm here, you want me to go in?" he questions, his stern daddy voice clearly prominent right now.

"No. I'll be there in just a minute, just focus on Lana?"

"Yeah, always." He grunts. "What do you want to do?"

I blow out a breath as I turn down the long driveway into Serenity, barely waiting for the gate to open before I'm driving through it. "Nothing. When I get there, I need you to take Lana home and let me handle it."

"You're sure?" he questions, and I growl.

"Positive. I'm pulling up now. I've got this, Trent."

I hang up and run onto the porch that wraps around the cabin, meeting him and Lana at the door. She looks so fucking scared, and I hate that I ended up putting her in this situation.

When I pull her into a tight hug, she hiccups against my chest. "I'm sorry," she whispers, and I pull back, shaking my head.

"You have nothing to be sorry for. I shouldn't have left her alone, and I'm sorry for putting you in this situation."

"Not your fault. Not anyone's fault," Trent says,

pulling my sister aside. "I've got Lana. You go help Abigail."

"Thanks." I give him a nod and push inside, closing the door behind me and heading to her room. "Abbs?" I call her name.

No response.

"Abigail," I call again, adding some steel to my voice this time.

"Go away, D," she says quietly, sounding exhausted and broken.

"Can't do that, sweetness, and I think you know that. Open the door."

"No."

"I have no issues breaking it down, so it's your call. I know you're upset right now, but you cannot be alone." I'm trying to be patient and supportive, but I will not let her go through this alone again.

When she doesn't respond, I pinch the bridge of my nose and remind myself that littles and middles need patience and soft tones. If I scare her, she will most likely get worse.

"I'll give you to the count of ten, sweetness, before I do what neither of us really wants me to do," I say quietly, and she huffs.

I hear her shuffling around before the door whips open, showing me the absolute destruction she's made of her room. "Are you too thick to get that I need some alone time?!" she snaps angrily.

I'll let that one slide because she's clearly distraught. "On the contrary, sweetness," I say, pushing myself into the room before she can slam it in my face. "I'm smart enough to deduce what happened while I was away."

Her face grows red then crumbles as she steps back, stumbling over everything before crashing to the bed. "I'm sorry I ruined the bedroom. I'll clean it up," she whispers, almost like she's afraid of me, and it stops me from advancing.

"I don't care about the room, Abbs. I care about you," I tell her gently.

"I—I don't think I can do this, D," she says, her voice breaking.

"Do what? What happened?" I take a step toward her and she flinches. "I would never hurt you, Abbs. Not fucking ever." And that's a goddamn promise.

"I know. I... it's a reflex."

"I get that. Can I come closer?" I ask her permission, knowing she needs to feel like she's in control right now.

When I spoke to Derek before Abigail moved in with me, he told me that self-harmer's often feel like they've lost control of everything in their life, but they can control how they let their emotions leave their system. They can control when they cut and how deep, and that if she was to relapse, I need to make sure she knows she has as much control as she needs.

"Yeah," she whispers, and I move slowly until I'm kneeling on the floor before her. "I don't know what happened."

Taking her hands in mine, I hold them tight, showing her I'm here and she can use my strength to get through this. "I'm right here, sweetness."

"You already know... don't you?" she whispers, meeting my gaze with tears running down her cheeks.

"Yeah, baby, I do."

# CHAPTER 23
# ABIGAIL

OF COURSE, HE KNOWS. I'M A FUCKING WRECK AND terrified his sister after I destroyed the room and locked her out. God, I feel like a fucking failure.

"What happened?" he asks me again, squeezing my hands tight, and I lean into his strength.

"You left, so I figured I would try and study," I answer him honestly. "But I couldn't focus and then I started to panic, I guess?" Blowing out a breath and shaking my head, I continue. "When I got up to try and distract myself, I just got... angry."

"Why angry?" he asks, moving to sit beside me on the bed.

I know I shouldn't, but I lean into his side and breathe a sigh of relief when he wraps his arm around me. This is something I've never had before. This comfort and safe feeling after a spell, but I am so glad he's here right now.

"Because I know that my brain needs time to heal, yet I can't stop myself from pushing too hard. It's like graduating has become this obsession and I'm losing my mind because I haven't met the goal I've set for myself."

It's not an easy thing for me to admit, but I *have* been obsessing over it. I know I need time to heal and that my brain needs longer than the rest of my body to get back to normal, but I can't stop. I've been telling myself for so long that I had to graduate by a certain date, and now I feel this anxious panic building inside of me.

"Sweetness, you have no reason to be angry with yourself. You're doing incredible right now, and that guidance counsellor had no right to message you," he says sternly, and I nod.

"Logically, I know that. All of it, but I can't," I sigh, "I have this feeling in my gut that something terribly wrong is going to happen if I don't graduate now."

Dameon pulls me closer, and I snuggle into his chest, letting the tears fall. I wouldn't want to be anywhere but here in his arms and this place where I'm safe and cared for, yet the fear follows me still. I hate it.

"Can I ask you something?" D asks, stroking my hair to calm me down.

"Yeah, sure." I feel so tired, and my arms hurt. It took more than one or two slices to feel any form of relief this time because I let myself get so out of control. I really need to clean them up, but I'm ashamed right now.

Until today, this has been the longest I've ever gone without cutting, and while I know it's not a straight road to recovery, I still feel like I've let everyone down, including myself.

"How long were you cutting before the accident?"

I take a deep breath and lean into him even more. I'm practically sitting in his lap at this point, but he doesn't seem to mind.

"Three years," I admit weakly. "Maybe a year now where they've been deep enough to leave scars."

Dameon sucks in a breath and his hold on me tightens before he's pulling back. When he's grabbed my chin in his hand, he lowers his forehead to mine before saying the last words I ever expected to hear.

"I'm so fucking proud of you, Abigail." A cries leaves me and I'd collapse if he wasn't holding me, his words washing over me like a soft blanket. "You've been fighting alone for so fucking long that you found a way to cope the only way you could. A way to survive instead of giving up when everything was so fucked up."

"I'm weak," I cry, and his eyes blaze with fire.

"No, you're one of the strongest people I've ever met. And don't argue with me because I know what struggling with mental health looks like, Abigail. But you don't have to fight this battle alone anymore."

I swallow the emotion clawing at my throat. "I don't know any other way. Nothing that Dr. Patrick has suggested is working, D."

"Have you given any thought to talking with Derek?" he asks, letting go of my chin and pulling away from my face. I feel the loss of his warmth and instantly want it back. I want so much from D right now, I don't even know where to begin.

"I think I want to try. Lana told me the other day that he's really helped her," I whisper. "Maybe he can help me as well."

What I don't tell D is that Lana also confided in me about her dynamic with Trent and how much it has helped her to heal. I can't say I'm surprised that she's a little because I know Rina is, but I never really looked into it much because it was none of my business.

When I asked Lana a bunch of questions, what did surprise me is how much I related to what she was saying. I understood how letting someone take over and make decisions for you could help get one into little space. A part of me even longed to feel what she was describing.

I want to feel like I can let go and let be. I want to be able to let the inner child inside of me blossom and grow, and forget the outside harshness of the world.

The more she talked, the more I realized that I may not be full-on little like her and Rina are, but I could very well be a middle or even liddle. I'm definitely drawn to things like colouring, even doing that with sheets I'd print out when I was at home. But I never thought anything of it. Plenty of adults colour for stress relief, right?

"I think he could definitely help you. Do you want to give him a call?" D asks me.

"I do, but I have something I need to do first," I tell him quietly, looking away in embarrassment.

"Does it involve cleaning your arms?" he asks me without an ounce of disgust, and I close my eyes, nodding. "Come on, I'll help, then we can go make some lunch."

God, I really am hungry, but I don't know how to feel about him helping me. "I don't—"

"If you're too uncomfortable with me seeing them, I will leave you be. But I won't judge you, sweetness. You have absolutely nothing to be afraid of when it comes to me."

I search his eyes for anything that might prove he doesn't want to do this and is just being nice, but I don't find anything to support that, so I find myself agreeing.

"Yeah. I, uh, I could really use some help. Please."

If I'm ever going to try to heal and maybe find my inner child, then I need to learn to accept help from others. This can be my first step in doing that. Maybe eventually I will get up enough courage to voice more of my needs.

"Good girl," he praises me, and I swear to fuck my heart flutters. He really needs to stop trying to make me melt.

And maybe I need to call Ted, because this attraction to D is dangerous. Even I know that if I'm going to rely on him to help me through this, I need to keep it platonic. So why does that thought feel almost wrong?

Fuck, I feel so lost. I need to text Lana and ask her some more questions later on.

# CHAPTER 24
# DAMEON

"Dameon, where are you heading this early?" Carl asks when I head outside.

Abby is spending the day with Trent and Lana, and finally getting her first riding lesson with Star outside of the stalls. She's a good horse and I know she won't hurt Abby, but I'm still concerned about her healing.

She finally went to see Richard yesterday, and honest to fuck it was hard to get her to agree. But he gave her a clean bill of health since she's been adhering to the study rules, and the migraines have eased up.

Of course, I also insisted on a few scans first which earned me the title of *'controlling and paranoid asshole'*. Honestly, and I will never tell her this, she's so fuck adorable when she grumbles, I don't even care that she's calling me names. As long as it's something her hidden little would call me and not some rude comment.

"I have to teach some people a lesson about decorum and human decency," I call over my shoulder.

"Just don't get arrested, yeah?" God, he's such a smartass.

"Just because you're the oldest, doesn't mean you're the wisest, brother." The smirk on my face is enough to have him rolling his eyes at me before turning serious.

"I'm serious, Dameon. Abigail needs you right now, so don't go doing something incredibly stupid."

I glare at him with as much heat as I can muster, which isn't a lot since he's looking out for her just as I'm doing.

"I need to talk to Principal Darvon and the new school counsellor," I state, and his eyes darken.

"That the prick who emailed her, stressing her out so much she had that breakdown last week?" When I dip my head, he growls. "Right. Well then, just don't get caught."

They don't know everything about Abigail's struggles, but they know enough. They know she's having a hard time with her mental health and that's all they really need to know. The rest is for Travis, the doctors, and myself to know and help her with. If she wants to tell others later, that's up to her, but it's no one else's business.

"Don't intend to, bro. I'll be back in a bit, but keep her occupied, yeah? And make her drink that shake," I ask, and climb into the truck.

"Damn, man. You've got it bad, don't you?" he jokes, but I can't tell him to go fuck himself because, well, I do.

I don't know what it is I feel for Abby yet, but I know it's not brotherly, and I know it's a lot more than friendship. But anything beyond that, all I can say is I'm protective as fuck over her.

"She needs to take care of herself," I say instead, and his eyes widen.

"Got it. I'll make sure she drinks the shake before she's allowed to see Star."

"Thank you."

"Anytime. If I ever fall for someone, I'm sure you'd do the same for me." He knows I would, but he's saying this as a reminder that we're brothers and family, and he'd do anything for an extension of any of us.

Because if you're close to any of us, you're

protected and cared for. Period. It's the way us East-on's roll.

"You fucking know it, man. Be back in a bit," I tell him before closing the door and taking off down the drive.

It's time to go teach this new bastard some manners.

*Haven Hills High.*

God, it's been almost a decade since I attended, but I know for a fact I wasn't a model student. Actually, the only one of us that was, was Lana. Straight A's, smart as a whip, and all around horse and book nerd, she laid low and never got into trouble.

Carl, Joe, and me? Well, the same can't be said for us. Hell, Trent went to school with Carl, and he wasn't a model student either, but the four of us definitely agreed on one thing no matter what. That was that we kept guys like us away from Lana.

The glare I get from the office secretary when I step inside is enough to know they haven't forgotten about the shit I pulled back then. Though, to be fair, I did accidentally light the science room on fire. And it actually was an accident, not that they believed me. The one time I was actually trying not to get in shit, I ended up in the deep end. Go fucking figure.

"Mr. Easton, to what do we owe the pleasure of this visit?" Mrs. Murphy drawls, eyeing me with suspicion.

The woman is a serious hardass and always has been, but I don't take it personally. Not now that I'm older and can actually respect her viewpoints on things. Honestly, we're all little shits as teenagers, especially Easton boys.

"Mrs. Murphy, so good to see you still around and fierce as ever." I can tell by the dry look she gives me that she is not buying what I'm selling, and fair. "I need to talk to principal Darvon."

"Can I ask what this is in regards to? It's not as though you have a student here," she replies curtly, and I nod.

"Obviously not, but I am in charge of caring for one. Abigail Davies."

The second I mention Abby's name, her eyes soften dramatically. She always had that look for Lana as well. This caring and motherly instinct that just kind of takes over.

"Abigail is staying with you?" When I nod, she continues. "I'll let Mr. Darvon know you're here. One moment please."

She leaves to walk down the hall for a brief moment before she comes back and waves me through.

"He's waiting for you in his office."

I shiver at her words as flashbacks of visiting the principals office way too often when I attended come back to me. "Yeah, I don't miss that line," I mutter, shaking my head, and she actually chuckles.

"Come in," Principal Darvon calls the moment he sees me walk up. "It's good to see you, Dameon. Outside of you needing to be disciplined, that is," he says with a smile, making me laugh.

"Tell me about it. I think I should have purchased stock in this school back then for the amount of time I spent in your office."

"Well, you've clearly grown up. What can I do for you, son?"

Oh, there's a lot you can do for me. I'm just not sure you're going to like it.

# CHAPTER 25
# DAMEON

HUGH DARVON ISN'T A BAD MAN, AND HONESTLY HE'S really good at running this school in a way that shows the students they're cared for. That they aren't just a means to a pay cheque or a burden to him, and I think he's the reason so many children like us and Abigail find a way to succeed.

But this new counsellor? Yeah, I can't say the same for that bastard, and he's lucky I'm talking to Hugh and not him. "Actually, I came to speak to you about Abigail. I'm sure you were made aware that she was recently injured and in recovery?" I question, and his shoulders slump.

"I did hear, and I'm sorry Miss Davies was hurt," he says tersely, trying to keep the anger from his face.

Haven Hills is a small town. Travis chose not to make anything public for Abby's safety, but when the mayor gets arrested the same night his only child is admitted to the hospital in dire condition, well... news spreads fast. I'm sure everyone has heard snippets of the truth mixed with a lot of rumours, but none of that matters in the grand scheme of things. The only thing that matters is that all of us surrounding Abby keep her safe.

"I'm going to level with you here," I tell him, leaning forward and resting my forearms on my thighs.

"Please do."

"I'm sure there are a lot of rumours flying around about this and that when it comes to Mayor Davies and Abby." When he doesn't say anything, I know I'm right. "I don't give a flying fuck about anything that anyone else is saying. What I do care about is that no one stresses Abby while she's in recovery, and it's my duty to make sure of that."

"Yes, of course. I had heard she was staying at Serenity now that she's out of the hospital. But what does that have to do with me, Dameon?" he questions, looking confused. "Abigail is welcome back at any time, but I don't want her pushing herself. From what I've heard, she needs a lot of time to recover both mentally and physically."

"You'd have heard right," I tell him, sitting back up straight. "But apparently someone in your school doesn't have the same feelings, and in contacting her, he's caused a lot of stress." I shake my head. "I won't be getting into any details, but I will say this. If this person values their life, you will make sure they are nowhere near this school when she does come to write her final exam."

"Hold on," he says, holding up a hand. "First of all, death threats will not be tolerated in any form, and I will call the sheriff if you speak that way again." Oh look, he's mad, but so the fuck am I. "Secondly, I don't know what you're even referring to, so maybe instead of jumping to violence you could tell me what the hell you're talking about," he spits out, and I'm momentarily shocked.

I don't think I've ever seen him lose his temper before.

When he came to Haven Hills High fifteen years ago, he was in his mid thirties and cool as a cucumber. Nothing, and I really do mean nothing, broke his calm exterior, so this is a new side to him. Or maybe it's because I'm no longer a student.

"Your guidance counsellor emailed Abigail not

too long ago about needing to do her exam. He made sure to point out that this was *her* requested timeline and that she needed to adhere to it." He curses, and runs his hands down his face as I continue. "This email sent her into a relapse and I will not tolerate someone hurting her in any way, Hugh. Ever." I say it with such fierceness he's momentarily taken aback.

I watch as he picks up the phone without saying a word to me. "Rachel, could you send Billings down here please?" he asks, then hangs up and looks at me. "I can assure you, Dameon, I was unaware of this and I'm going to rectify the situation immediately."

"Thank you. And I apologize for my earlier statement, but you have to understand something. There is a lot more going on with Abigail than almost anyone knows, including Rose. I can't have this type of thing continuing to make her spiral and putting her health at risk."

"No, absolutely not. But there are less violent ways to discuss things, so just remain calm when he gets here or I will have Sheriff Colt called, understand?"

"I do," I state as there's a knock on the door.

"Come in," Hugh says. His tone is much more

authoritative than it was with me, and I'm glad he's taking this seriously.

"You wanted to see me, Principal Darvon?" the man asks as he enters before his eyes land on me. Confusion is clear on his face and I understand that. He has no idea who I am or just how badly he's pissed me off.

"Yes, Billings, please sit down." Hugh gestures to the chair beside me. "I'd like to discuss a student with you," he states once Billings is seated.

"Of course," he says, his eyes sliding over to me. "May I ask which student we're discussing?"

"I'm sure you recall our conversation about a Miss Abigail Davies when you joined our school a couple of months ago?" Hugh says to him, his eyes flicking to me quickly before landing back on his employee.

"Of course. She's the one that wanted to graduate early and had made every move to do so," Billings states. "But I'm sorry to report that I think she's changed her mind."

"Excuse me?" I bark, barely containing my anger. This mother fucker has a lot of balls to think Abby just quit on her goals. I'd like to give him a concussion as severe as hers was and see how well he does at trying to study.

"I'm sorry. Who are you?" he asks me with an attitude, and I swear I'm going to fucking lose it.

"Your worst fucking—"

"Dameon! Jesus, would you sit down!" someone yells at me when they burst through the office door.

"Sheriff?" Principal Darvon says in surprise.

"Hey, Hugh. Sorry to bust in here, but I was given a heads up Dameon may lose his shit. Seems I got here just in time." Travis gives me a look before closing the door.

"No way Carl called you," I state, knowing for a damn fact my brother would be all for me knocking this little prick down a few pegs. Mind you, I did tell him I wouldn't get caught and here I am threatening the bastard in front of witnesses.

"Abby did," he says quietly, shocking the hell out of me. "She had a feeling you were heading down here and was able to work it out of Lana."

Well, fuck. It's not like I can be mad at either of them since this wasn't exactly a secret. I just didn't want to stress Abby out by mentioning the school or that fucking email again.

"Thanks for coming, Sheriff, but I think Dameon here was about to sit back down. Right, Mr. Easton?" Hugh all but orders, fully in principal mode now. Yeah, this feels familiar. Now I feel like I'm in high school again. Except for the fact I'm here to prevent something happening to my sweetness again.

"What the heck is going on?" Billings asks, looking between all of us, but I ignore him and focus on Travis.

"It's good you're here since you'll understand exactly what I mean when I say this, whereas these two don't. This tool," I point in Billings' direction, "caused Abigail to relapse last week."

"Fuck," Travis hisses, running his hand down his face to compose himself. "Okay, I get why you're pissed. I am too." He shoots the asshole counsellor a glare that has him withering in his seat like the weaselly prick he is. "But you can't come onto school grounds and start barking threats at people. Jesus, man."

"Then tell him to keep his mouth shut about her until he knows why the fuck he was called down here in the first place!" I snap, and Travis sighs.

"Hugh, what happened?"

"It appears Billings missed the memo that Abigail had been in an accident and was taking medical time off before completing her final exam." He shoots Billings a look of pure frustration.

"What? What memo?" Billings sputters.

"The one that went to every educator inside this

school and even to our board of education stating that Abigail Davies needed time to recover from her injuries, and that no one was to bother her. That she would reach out to us when she had the all-clear from her doctors to return to school," Hugh explains, and the colour drains from Billings' face.

"Sir, I—I didn't know."

"Do you make it a habit of ignoring emergency correspondence, then?" Travis is the one to ask the question, and I swear the weasel shits himself.

"No. No! I swear. I just—I don't know how I missed that."

"Abigail's health is not something to toy with, Mr. Billings," Travis warns. "Your mistake has set her back, and I will not tolerate that, you hear me? That girl has been through enough."

"I—"

"Billings, this states you opened the email." Hugh waves at his computer. "We'll discuss the repercussions of going against direct orders from doctors and legal authority where a student's health is concerned," he warns him.

"Yes, sir," Billings says. His jaw is tight like he's fighting anger, and I'm about a second away from showing him what real anger looks like when Hugh speaks again.

"As far as Abigail is concerned, thank you for bringing this to my attention, Dameon. I can promise you she has all of the time she needs, and we will be ready when she is. Furthermore, I will make absolutely certain that Abigail goes directly through Rachel and myself when that time comes."

I nod stiffly, standing and shaking his hand. "Thank you, Principal Darvon. I appreciate that." I refuse to look at the other fucker as Travis says a quick goodbye and we leave the school.

I'm beyond ready to get back to Abby right fucking now.

"Hey, hold on," Travis snarls and grabs my arm. "I know you run hot most of the time, and I get that you're protective of Abby, but you can't go around just threatening people. She needs you, Dameon, and goddammit, if I have to arrest you and let that girl down, I'll beat your ass."

His words are like a bucket of ice water. "I'd never let her down."

He nods and lets go of my arm. "Then keep the anger out of it when dealing with shit like that next time." He points back to the school. "It's called being diplomatic. And if you're going to threaten someone, which I do not recommend, for fuck's sake, don't do it where there are witnesses!"

"You're right, I'm sorry. I just... you didn't see her, Travis. She was a wreck."

He scowls back at the school like even he wants to storm back in there and strangle the fucker who set her off. "Just take care of her, Dameon. And if you can't be diplomatic, take Trent."

I snort and shake my head before saying goodbye and getting in the truck.

Yeah, I won't be asking Trent to handle shit like this. I can do it, and I was mostly fine until he started talking about her in a negative way. That is something I will not tolerate. Not toward Abby, not toward my sister. And not toward any woman or little that ever comes under our protection.

# CHAPTER 26
## ABIGAIL

OKAY, I CAN DO THIS. I MEAN, I MET WITH DR. Patrick and told him everything, so the sheriff's brother should be easy-peasy, right? Right.

Taking another deep breath, I use the new laptop D bought me—insisting I needed it for school—to click the button, taking me to the secured video call.

While I wait for it to dial, I think back to yesterday. It was amazing. Getting outside to walk with Star was both exhilarating, and as crazy as it sounds, it was freeing.

It didn't matter that I wasn't actually riding her, it still felt incredible to just imagine. And thank fuck, because the anxiety I felt until D came back in one piece was intense. I just knew he was going to do something stupid if I hadn't called the Sheriff —Travis.

"Abigail? Abigail, are you alright?" a voice breaks me from my thoughts, and I jump.

"H-hi," I croak, my heart racing. I really need to stop zoning out. At least the migraines have disappeared since D enforced Dr. Evans' rules, but zoning out is still a bad habit.

"Hi." The man smiles. "Are you okay?" he asks in a gentle voice.

He seems kind, and he looks enough like Travis to put me at ease a little. He's well dressed with a neat beard and dark hair, with striking blue eyes that smile with him.

He's everything Lana said he'd be and then some. There's just something about the way he seems so at ease in his own skin that it radiates through the screen to help you feel more comfortable... as crazy as that sounds.

"Yeah, hi. I'm sorry." I shake my head, feeling my cheeks heat from embarrassment. "I got lost in my head."

Wow. I am talking way too much. Why am I opening up to him so easily?

He smiles and nods. "It's okay. I get lost in my

head too sometimes. It's completely normal." He winks, making me giggle.

Okay, what the fuck? Am I sick? I don't giggle. Ever.

*Unless you're letting that inner little out that you believe you have.*

I guess I could be, but now is a weird time for her to shine through. Shit, at this rate, the man is going to think I'm certifiable before he even gets through the first session.

"I'm sorry," I rush out, and he holds his hand up with a smile. God, it's no wonder he puts Lana and Rina both at ease if he's this patient and understanding with them.

"There is no need to apologize, Abigail. It's okay, and believe me when I say that many of my clients do the same thing," he reassures me, and I feel my shoulders relax. "Now, how are you doing?" he asks, and I know we're back to all business now.

I talk to him about my past and how Mom died. I try to tell him the things that my father did over the years, but it's too much all at once so he makes me stop and move onto something else, asking me about Rose.

"It sounds like you're very lucky to have her in your life," he says once I've finished gushing about my best friend. "Do you think you're ready to talk about your coping mechanism?"

I suck in a breath and close my eyes, and my hands immediately go to my forearms still covered in bandages. There's no need for them to still be there, but Dameon insisted on it because he's worried about infection. Honestly, the man needs a chill pill. This isn't my first rodeo, but for the first time in a long time, I'm hoping it will be one of my last.

I'm not naive enough to think I'll never relapse again, but I have hope that I can heal and find better ways of dealing with the pain and overwhelm.

Like being little, but that will also involve having someone to be my caregiver too. I've done a lot of research since Lana and I spoke, and she even said that her and Trent were meant to start out as strictly platonic, so I know that's a possibility. Maybe, if I can find someone I trust enough.

I have one person in mind, but I'm not so sure he's the right fit given everything I've ever heard about him, but it's worth bringing up at some point if I can keep my attraction toward him out of it.

God, I really need to get laid.

"I think so," I say, answering Derek's question. "What is it you want to know?"

"That's a good question. I'm not here to judge you in any way, and I need you to know that before I respond. Can you tell me you understand that this is a judgement free space?" His voice takes on a more stern tone that reminds me of Travis, and I find myself sitting up straighter.

"I'll do my best?" I wince when it comes out as a question. "I struggle with this and how it makes me feel."

Derek writes some things down on his notepad and looks back at me. "What is the part you struggle with the most? In terms of others knowing, I mean."

I blow out a breath and look up to the ceiling, trying to form an explanation that will make sense to someone who has never gone through this before. Not that I know for certain he hasn't, but I hope he hasn't.

"The way people will view me, I guess?" I frown. "I don't want people to view me as weak or pity me because my way of coping isn't the societal norm," I state, and he makes some more notes.

"That's an interesting perspective. Referring to it as outside of the societal norm. What do you mean by that?"

"Dad was an alcoholic. Some people do drugs, some run, some binge eat or go to the other extreme.

All of these things are just as detrimental to one's health, but they're often less frowned upon in a way. It's like... all of the things I've mentioned, people are able to wrap their heads around it easier than someone who hurts themselves to feel better. Who makes themselves bleed," I whisper, and he jots more things down.

"I can certainly see where you'd feel that way, and to a certain degree, you'd be right." His answer surprises me. "But I feel like adverse reactions to cutting have more to do with the idea of inflicting the harm onto themselves rather than the act itself. Does that make sense?" He shakes his head. "In simpler terms, I think people react badly because the act of cutting themselves open is something they fear. They can't open their minds to look past their fear of pain to see how it may be healing for someone else."

Wow. That actually makes a lot of sense. I'm not sure I ever would have thought of it from that perspective before.

"So, you think that their feelings of pity aren't greater than they are for other chosen ways of coping, it just comes across harsher because of their own fears?" I ask, making sure I understand what he's saying.

"Exactly. No one wants to think of someone they know drinking themselves to death or overdosing on drugs. They don't want to see them die of a heart attack from too much food or too little. And they don't want to see their loved ones making themselves bleed, but the former options don't become as terrifying right from the start as cutting does. Not most of the time anyway," he explains, and I get it.

Fuck, I lived it. Dad didn't start hurting me immediately after Mom died. He was always drinking, but his aggression and abuse wasn't instantaneous. It happened over time the same way my scars multiply over time. The only difference being mine are seen right away. The second that blade cuts through the skin, the evidence of my coping is there for the eye to see.

"Wow," I whisper, not sure what else to say.

"It's a lot to think about," Derek says, and I nod numbly. "Why don't you take some time to think on that, and we can meet up again when you're ready. If you'd like to?" he asks, not wanting to assume anything.

"Is there any chance you have some time to talk tomorrow? I have something else I'd like to ask about, but I don't think my brain can handle anymore information right now," I tell him honestly, and he smiles.

"I can't tomorrow because I'm working at the hospital, but how about the following morning?"

"Thank you. That sounds great. And thanks for helping me see this a different way," I say, feeling a bit lighter. "I think it helped a lot."

"Good. Sometimes we just need someone to show us a different path. Just because we can't see them, doesn't mean they aren't there, it just means we aren't familiar with the terrain. Yeah?"

I smile. "I like that. Thanks, Dr. Colt."

He winces and shakes his head. "Please, call me Derek." When I look surprised, he chuckles. "If you were a client in my office without being connected to Serenity, I'd insist on the formality, but not there. The entire goal behind Serenity Stables being altered to a safe place for people in danger and or need means making them comfortable."

"Wow." It's all I've got at the moment with my brain overflowing with so many different things.

"Have a good evening, Abigail. I'll talk to you soon."

"Definitely, and same to you. Goodnight."

Once I'm back in my room, I shoot off a message to meet up with Ted to blow off some steam. As much as I want to talk to Dameon about him teaching me how to live in the lifestyle, I need to get rid of the nervousness coursing through me. Sex helps with that.

That, and maybe if I get laid I'll stop thinking about how hot Dameon is because that can never happen. Right?

## CHAPTER 27
## DAMEON

ME:

Thanks for making room in your
schedule today, man.

DEREK:

Anytime. I'm glad to help anyone,
you know that.

ME:

Have a good night.

DEREK:

You too.

ABIGAIL TOLD ME ABOUT THEIR CALL OVER DINNER.
She didn't get into the specifics, and honestly, it's
none of my business. Even if she were my woman,

her therapy is *hers*. If she wants to talk about it, I'm here. If not, that's cool too. As long as she doesn't shut me out.

She seemed lighter tonight, so I'm hopeful that Derek was able to help her feel at ease. With time, I feel like she'll be well on her way to feeling more and more herself without the heaviness of what that bastard has done to her over the years.

After dinner, we chatted for a bit while we cleaned up the kitchen together, then she said she was tired and going to bed. I didn't question it, given the headaches she's been having, but I do feel lonely.

I've gotten pretty used to having Abby in my space now, and suddenly I'm wondering what the hell I did before she arrived.

Just as I'm about to give into the tiredness from working on the ranch today, the alarm system on the house goes off, making me fly out of bed.

"Abby!" I holler, barrelling down the hallway. When I reach her door, it's locked and I can't get it. "Abigail! Abby, talk to me!"

"Jesus! Make it stop!" I hear her screech over the alarm, and wince.

Running to the front door, I disable the alarm

and grab the gun I keep hidden just in case, and make my way back to her room.

"Abbs?" I ask again, my heart still racing.

"I'm sorry!" she cries and the door flies open. "I'm sorry, okay! I didn't know the whole goddamn house was booby-trapped!"

Confusion runs through me as my brain tries to catch up to what's happened. I'm still stuck on the fucking alarm sounding, so it doesn't click until I see her window open and realize she's dressed in a dark hoodie and pants.

"You we're trying to sneak out?" I ask slowly. When I try to slide the gun into my jeans, it's then I realize I'm only in my boxers.

Fucking hell.

"I didn't realize I was a prisoner," Abby snaps at me, looking both angry and embarrassed.

"Abbs, what? You're not a prisoner." What is she talking about?

"Then why is my room rigged to notify the entire fucking state?!"

"Umm, it's not just your room, Abbs. It's every room in every cabin and building on the property," I explain.

I've definitely caught up to the fact she was

trying to sneak out of the house, and I'm very curious to know why.

"What? What the fuck for?" she asks me angrily, and I sigh.

"So that whoever we're keeping here under the radar is safe. You can open the windows just fine, but they're rigged with sensors that are triggered if there's weight put on the frame. That way, if someone were to find Serenity and get past the security measures we have in place, then they still won't get into the buildings without us knowing."

Her face falls and tears build in her eyes. "So it's not just my room," she states. "Fuck, I feel like an idiot."

Yeah, no. I'm not putting up with that. "You're not an idiot, Abbs. But I am curious, why were you trying to sneak out at eleven at night?" I question just as the others barge through the front door.

"Dameon? Abigail?! Everything alright?" Carl calls as he walks further into the house.

"Yeah, false alarm." I eye Abigail for a moment and decide they don't need to know that she was trying to sneak off. "Abbs triggered the sensor when she leaned over too far and put her weight on the window frame."

Her eyes shoot up to mine. They're filled with

thanks for not telling everyone the truth, but she shouldn't be thanking me. I'm still going to get to the bottom of why she was sneaking out.

"I didn't think they were that sensitive," Trent says as they make their way to me. "Oh come on, man. Put some fucking pants on."

"Hey, it's my house and this woke me up too, so deal with it. I'm going back to bed as soon as I get this reset. And they're not, I just forgot to tell Abby they were there so she didn't know not to out too much weight on them," I explain, and they nod.

"So, false alarm? Everyone is good?" Carl checks again, looking from Abby to me, and we both nod.

"Good. Tired, but safe. Wait, where's Lana?" I'm surprised she's not with us where Trent can watch over her after the alarms went off.

"In the panic room. I'm going to head back. She's scared, but safe." Trent waves goodbye and leaves.

"I just text Joe. He's calling Travis and telling him it was a false alarm and not to bother coming out," Carl tells me. "I'm going back to the house. I have a call with Trent's partner first thing in the morning."

"Sorry," Abby apologizes, and Carl gives her a warm smile.

"It's not a problem, little one. Get some sleep. I'm just grateful everyone is safe."

Okay, I know he didn't mean to call her little one, but I'm ready to strangle the jackass. She's not his, goddammit. She's mine.

*Whoa. You're not a daddy, Dameon. Get your shit together, man.*

I follow him back out, setting the system up again and turning it on once the door is locked, then make my way back to her.

"I'm tired," Abigail whispers when I step back into the room. "Can I go to bed please?"

"Oh, sweetness. It's cute you think we're going to skip past the real reason the alarms went off." I move over to the bed and sit down beside her. "Why were you trying to sneak out, Abbs?"

She sighs dramatically like this whole thing has ruined her entire life, and it's a reminder that she's probably in little or middle space. I can't say it's just her normal teenage reaction because Abigail isn't normal. She doesn't react in a dramatic fashion like most her age would.

"It doesn't really matter. It was an idiotic plan anyway," she says, picking up her phone and typing something to someone.

There's a large part of me that wants to snatch it from her, but that would be an overreaction to how she's behaving. "I don't ask a lot, Abigail, but I do ask for respect." I use my Dom voice and her eyes shoot up to mine immediately.

"What?"

"You're texting someone while I'm trying to talk to you about something serious." I point to her phone, and her eyes widen before she drops it onto the bed.

"Sorry. Just habit," she states, and I believe her.

"I accept your apology. Now, considering you weren't using the front door or telling me you wanted to go out, I'm going to guess you were trying to do something you figured I wouldn't approve of," I mention, taking a wild guess. It wasn't so long ago that I was doing the same type of shit.

Her face flushes crimson as she looks away, and heat rises up inside of me like someone flicked a switch. A blush like that can really only mean one thing, and that's that she was trying to sneak out to meet a guy.

"D, can we not?" she asks, and I growl, moving closer and grip her chin, bringing her face close to mine.

"You were sneaking out to meet up with a guy?" I ask, and her breath catches. I don't miss the way her pupils dilate as she looks into my eyes.

"It doesn't matter," she breathes out.

"Oh, sweetness. On the contrary, it matters a whole fucking lot." I drop my eyes to her lips, fighting myself to not give in.

God, I want to. I want to kiss her lips hard enough to bruise them so she never thinks about another guy again. And the look in her eyes mixed with her body language says she wants me to do the same, but I can't. I really fucking can't.

There are so many things we need to discuss before I could ever make that move, and I don't even know if she's ready for what I am and what I need. And more importantly, I don't know that I could be what she needs.

Do I have the ability to be a daddy and caregiver to that degree? Taking care of my sister is one thing, but adding attraction and sex into things would be a whole different field. But I'm getting way ahead of myself here.

## CHAPTER 28
## ABIGAIL

Fuck. How is it that he's able to make me feel like this? Is it what real attraction is meant to feel like? Because right now I feel like I'm burning from the inside out.

"It doesn't," I tell him again, holding his eyes with mine.

The fact that I tried, and failed, to sneak out isn't even bothering me outside of the embarrassment. I mean, Jesus, the entire fucking calvary came busting into my bedroom because I wanted to have a quick fuck.

I literally woke everyone on the ranch up because I'm an idiot. That kind of shit kills the libido. Or you'd think it would, but having Dameon this close to me in only a pair of boxers? Jesus fuck, I can only take so much.

"It fucking does, Abigail," he growls, his eyes moving back to my lips as his grip on my chin tightens.

I hold my breath when he leans in closer, moving his hand to the back of my neck. It's like he knows I'd freak out if he gripped the front. I used to enjoy that kind of thing with Ted before Dad choked me to near death with his belt.

Ted never did it to cut off air, but just the idea of it being a possibility used to turn me on. Now it's a thing from my own personal nightmares.

"D," I breathe against his lips. God, they're so close to mine I can almost feel them.

"Abbs," he groans, closing his eyes. I can see the war playing out on his face. He's doubting whether or not being with me is a good idea, and I hate it.

"Kiss me, D," I whisper, leaning in the rest of the way and grazing his lips with my own.

"Fuck!" he barks, losing the fight as his mouth crashes to mine in the hottest kiss I've ever had.

I moan into him and he takes the opening, pushing his tongue past my lips and grazing against my own, stealing the air from my lungs. "Yes," I whimper.

"Christ," he bites my lip, pushing me back onto the bed and moving to tower over me as his mouth continues to devour mine until I swear I may cum just like this, I'm so worked up.

I whimper, moving my hands to his chest and digging my nails into his flesh, lifting my hips when he growls against the pain.

"Fuck. No," he rasps, pulling away like he's been burned. He's off the bed before I can even process what's happening. "Jesus Christ." He's panting as much as I am, the evidence of how badly he wants me, tenting his boxers.

Holy mother of fuck. Dameon Easton is packing.

"D—what?" I ask, sitting up and shaking my head as what just happened comes into clarity.

"Abby, I'm so fucking sorry. Fuck!"

Ouch, that stings. "Dameon, get out," I tell him sternly, refusing to look him in the eye. I just kissed the man who finds my very existence annoying. Why the hell did I think he'd react any differently.

"Abbs, hold on," he says gently, and I shake my head. "We have to talk about this."

"No, we really fucking don't. Get. Out." Gah, I feel so stupid right now.

"No, sweetness, I won't. Not until we talk about

why I pulled away," he says sternly, and I scoff, swinging my eyes back to his.

"You pulled away because you can't stand me. I'm the bane of your existence, Dameon. I'm not a fucking idiot."

"Don't you dare," he growls, walking back over to me and kneeling on the floor in front of me so I have to look down at him. "Are you a royal pain in my ass? Fuck yes, you are, but that doesn't mean I don't fucking want you, Abbs. Fucking hell, baby, I want you so goddamn bad."

Swallowing the emotion in my throat, I stare down at him. "Liar," I say quietly, not even sure if I believe my own words. "You kissed me because I was going out to get laid and you got jealous. That's all this was."

"Oh, sweetness, it was so much more than jealousy." He shakes his head as his face darkens with pure hunger. "Abbs, you've been under my skin for years and I didn't know why until recently. Until I almost fucking lost you," he rasps, making tears spring to my eyes.

"I—"

"No, let me finish. Please?" he pleads, so I nod, and he takes my hands in his. "The second Travis said he was going to take you back to his place, I almost strangled the bastard. I didn't... no, I couldn't, let anyone else care for you but me. You're under my skin so deep, baby, I'll never get you out. But there is so much you don't know. So much we have to take into consideration before we can move forward."

Dameon takes a deep breath and continues. "First of all, your health is always going to be of the utmost importance to me, and I'm not sure you're ready for a relationship yet." When I go to argue, he gives me a look that stops me in my tracks. "Secondly, there is a lot about me that I'm sure you've heard rumours of, and it's a very serious conversation we're going to need to have before we can move forward with anything else.

"And thirdly, I have some suspicions about you, and I'm really fucking worried I won't be able to give you what you need. But if anyone can bring that out in me, it's you."

Is he saying what I think he's saying? God, I feel so overwhelmed with everything right now.

"You look exhausted and overwhelmed, sweetness. I think we should continue this conversation in the morning, but I *need* you to know that this isn't about not wanting you."

"Promise?" I ask, not even believing I'm letting

myself be so vulnerable right now when everything feels so raw.

"Promise, sweetness." He stands and kisses my forehead, making me melt. "You okay?" he asks, and I actually laugh.

"Define okay. I triggered alarms that are more intense than the damn Whitehouse and woke everyone up because I was trying to sneak out for a quick fuck." I slap my hand over my mouth the second I say it, but it's too late.

"Oh, don't worry. That conversation is definitely not over," he says darkly. "As far as waking everyone up, no one else knows why they were triggered."

"You lied to your family. For me..."

D smirks. "Technically, it wasn't a lie. I did forget to tell you we had top of the line security for every possible precaution. I just omitted something that had the potential to upset you. It's my job to protect you, Abigail, and that means from anything."

I can see the unspoken meaning in his eyes. He's worried that this might set me back and cause another relapse. If I'm being honest, I'm worried it might if I'm left alone to my thoughts. That's why the next question comes out of my mouth before I have a chance to second guess myself.

"Can you... will you sleep in here tonight?" I ask

him, sounding smaller than I've ever heard myself before.

He watches me for a moment, taking in the change in me before nodding. "Sure, sweetness. Just let me go grab some pants and my bedding."

I shake my head. "No. I promise I'll be good just, please hold me? I'm feeling odd and I don't want to be alone." I look at the floor as I admit this last part. "You're my safe space, D. Please?"

"Okay, sweetness. Anything for you."

## CHAPTER 29
## DAMEON

Fuck, she's beautiful when she sleeps. I wish I could hold her like this all day, but I need to get out of bed and make breakfast before she wakes up with my dick poking her in the ass.

Goddamn thing has a mind of its own when it comes to being close to her.

I don't even know how I went from saying nothing would ever happen between us to finding her attractive and now considering our options. Fuck, once we discuss the dynamics of this lifestyle, she still needs to figure out how she feels about it before we can move forward. And as much as I want to kiss her senseless and claim her as mine right here and now, I can't and it sucks.

Abby needs time to figure out who she is without

her father looming over her and threatening abuse. She needs to discover her little and do research to see what she wants to try and what she wants to stay firmly away from.

So while we may not be able to be together yet, maybe I can still guide her. I can help her find herself and her own path, teach her what she deserves and to look out for red flags. I can show her how a Dominant is supposed to, and should, treat her. This way, if her and I never take it past that kiss, at least I will know she's equipped with the knowledge she needs to not be taken advantage of.

"Stay in bed, Abbs," I whisper, hoping she doesn't wake up.

After a moment of making sure she's still breathing evenly, I gently unwrap myself from the woman in my arms and get out of bed.

Looking around, I find a notepad and pen to scribble a note on, leaving it beside her pillow.

*Gone to make breakfast. Rest as long as you need.*

*- D*

I scoff at myself for signing the goddamn thing. It's not like anyone else is getting into this house, but something tells me it will comfort her to see it rather than just the note.

By the time I've showered and changed, it's been a half hour since I left Abby, and I would love nothing more than to climb back into bed with her. But if I do that, I can't promise to be the gentleman I'm trying so fucking hard to be right now. Just getting out of there this morning without her feeling my morning wood was enough temptation for one day.

*Breakfast.* We need some food, and bacon makes everything better.

Grabbing the griddle that Carl bought me as a gag gift—unbeknownst to him, this thing fucking rocks—I heat it up while grabbing the eggs and bacon from the fridge.

"Fuck, that smells good," Abby mumbles as she pads into the kitchen.

The fact that the smell of bacon is what woke her up has me smiling like an idiot. I flip the eggs and lower the heat before turning around to face her.

She's still in her hoodie and leggings from last night, and fuck if she doesn't look cute.

"Language," I scold, and it earns me one of her famous eye rolls.

"Yeah, okay," she scoffs. "I'll mind my language when you mind yours." She smirks, and I lift an eyebrow.

"Little girls shouldn't swear." It's a risk to mention this before breakfast, but the heat in her cheeks makes me feel ten feet tall.

I've been thinking about her being a little or middle since I woke up this morning. Actually, since Travis brought it up to me while she was in the hospital. I've come to the conclusion that I can be what she needs because what she needs is me.

Abby needs a partner and daddy that's willing to be stern with her while helping her blossom into herself. A daddy that's going to take her sass in stride while still guiding her on what is and isn't appropriate.

"You think I'm a little?" she asks quietly, lifting her eyes to meet mine.

"I think you're you, and I think you have little tendencies." I move to plate our breakfasts, carrying them to the island and sitting beside her. "I'm not really sure how much you know about this lifestyle, Abbs. I'm going to need you to guide me," I tell her.

She swallows nervously, moving the food around on her plate. "I've talked to Lana and done a lot of research. Not as much as I want to because of the headaches. Studying has been my main goal, you know?"

I nod, looking at our plates. "Something is missing. Orange juice. We need OJ and water," I state.

Once I've gotten us both a glass of each, I sit back down and pick up my fork while she gulps down some OJ.

"How is that going? Studying, I mean." I point to her breakfast. "Eat first, then we can talk about the more intense things. You're too nervous."

Abby gives me a dry look that has me smirking despite myself. "Right, because I eat so well on a normal day."

So much sass.

"I know you struggle to eat breakfast, but try for me? Eating properly will help you focus later."

After a few bites, she turns to me. "It's going well. I actually think I'm ready, but I want to take a few more days just to make sure I'm not stressing myself out unnecessarily," she explains.

"Take all the time you need. I told you Principal

Darvon said for you to reach out to him when you're ready."

"Thanks for that, by the way. I'm glad I don't have to see anyone else. I just want to get in, take the exam, and get the fu—flip out."

I chuckle, shaking my head. "Good catch, sweetness, but you may be right about the swearing. And you're welcome. It was my pleasure to give that little shit a hard time."

"Hold up. Why can you swear and I can't? Double standard much?"

"You little. Me Dom, or Daddy. Whichever you'd prefer if we choose to go down that road." Well shit. So much for waiting until after breakfast.

"That's dumb," she whines, her voice taking on a higher pitch.

When her eyes widen, I can tell it surprises her, but I just smile.

"Hey, I don't make the rules," I smart off before stopping. "Actually, I do. Some of them, anyway. So maybe I'll allow big Abby to swear."

She snorts and takes the last bite of her food. "Oh, you're so full of it, D," she teases after swallowing.

Abby hops off her stool and backs away with a smirk on her face before I can grab her, and I know there's about to be the best type of trouble coming my way.

"You think you're the big bossy-boss pants." She sticks her tongue out and laughs, continuing to step away from me slowly.

Someone wants to play, huh? Okay, we can play first and talk later.

# CHAPTER 30
## ABIGAIL

I DON'T KNOW WHERE THIS ENERGY AND PLAYFULNESS is coming from, but I don't want to fight it. I feel so light and free right now, even as D prowls toward me slowly.

My heart races as he matches me step for step. I move back, he moves ahead. Is this what it's like to be little?

"My little girl is feeling playful, is she?" he taunts with a smirk, and I melt. Freaking hell, do I melt.

"Your little girl?" I squeak, freezing where I stand. I wasn't really sure Dameon was a Daddy Dom. Lana hinted she thought he might be, but she said it would take someone special to coax it out of him because he's not even aware of it.

It's silly to think I'm that person, right?

A look of desire and longing crosses his face before the predator is back, smirking at me like he's a devil in sheep's clothing.

"You bet your ass, sweetness." Fuck. Me. Sideways.

"There's that sword again!" I pout and stomp my foot.

What the hell was that? I stare down at my foot in complete and utter shock as my cheeks heat. I've never stomped my foot in my life.

"Did you just stomp your foot, baby?" Dameon coos, and I lift my wide eyes to meet his amused ones.

"Uh, yes? But also, no. Cause I has no clue where that came from," I mutter, still freaking baffled.

"Hmm, how to handle this," he says, stepping closer to me. "I could punish you for throwing a tantrum." My head snaps back to him, panic starting to build. "Hey, easy."

"I—I..."

"Abby, hey, look at me," he orders softly, and I do. This is where it would be pertinent to have our limits conversation, but there's a huge part of me that knows this will be over before it starts.

"I'm not who you need," I whisper, my chest aching as the words slip past my lips.

"Whoa, hold on. How did we get from playing to you thinking that? Was it because I mentioned punishments?" D asks, and I nod. "Okay, we need to sit down and have that talk sooner rather than later because I can't have you panicking like this, sweetness."

Dameon guides me over to the couch and sits down, pulling me into his lap until I'm straddling him, laying my head on his chest while he holds me tight.

"Talk to me, Abigail. What's going on in this head of yours?" he whispers, running his hand down my hair in a calming motion. God, he's good at this.

"I think this is a mistake," I tell him, pulling away. Or trying to, but he holds onto me tighter.

"Nope, sorry. That wasn't an answer. Answer me, Abigail. What's going on? Where is all of this coming from?"

I can hear the concern in his voice and it makes me feel like an asshole, but I'm scared. I'm scared to open myself up to him, knowing he needs more than I may ever be able to give him.

Feeling saddened and heavy, a complete contrast

of everything I felt moments ago when my little came out, I pull my head back to look up at him.

"I know what you're into, Dameon." A look of understanding crosses his face, but he remains silent, allowing me to continue. "I've heard about what you like to do with women." I shrug.

"Are you one to believe rumours, Abbs?" he questions me, and I shrug again.

"When enough women say it, it kind of means it's true. Doesn't it?" I challenge, meeting his gaze, and he sighs.

"I think you need to tell me exactly what you've heard, then we can go from there." D gives me a pointed look. "And then, when I correct those perceptions you have in your mind about the things you assume I need, we can have the talk about us. Yeah?"

Do I want to do this? It would be easier to just walk away, wouldn't it? At least then I wouldn't get hurt.

*Yeah, sure you wouldn't, Abigail. Though, at least it would be you breaking your own heart.*

"Wherever it is you just went, come back to me, sweetness," he coaxes me.

I blink and shake my head, focusing back on him. It's time to either nut up or shut up, I guess.

"Yeah, okay." I squirm on his lap, wishing I was sitting anywhere else for this conversation. "You're a sadist," I whisper, and he dips his head.

"I am."

"You like to hit women. Cause them pain."

A look of darkness washes over him, and he grips my hips tightly. "Okay, let's pause there." The sternness in his voice makes me shiver, but not in a bad way. "Everything that happens with any woman I've been with is always consensual. It is not abuse."

I swallow at the slight anger in his tone, but as scary as it is, I don't think he's mad at me. "I didn't say it was," I state, getting defensive.

"I would never lay my hand on a woman in a way that would truly hurt her, Abigail."

"Yeah, D, I know," I tell him, because I do know.

"What else have you heard?" he asks after a moment, and I feel my entire body flush with arousal.

Oh, I've heard that he's a sadist and gets off on doling out pain, but I've heard about the orgasms and pleasure he gives too. And that his dick is huge, which I kind of got to see last night.

"Oh, my baby is blushing. Now I need to know," he teases, his body relaxing.

"Nope. You really don't," I croak, making him

laugh. It's a deep and thoroughly delicious sound that reverberates through me, setting me on fire.

"I'll take it that the rest is all good." He smirks, using his hands to pull my core against him, making me gasp. "Christ," he groans when I slide against his growing erection.

"Oh," I moan, and something inside of him snaps.

D lunges forward, gripping my neck and taking my mouth with his in a passionate kiss that leaves no room for argument. With every stroke of his tongue against mine, he's laying claim to my very fucking soul, and I give it right back.

I rock against him as my arms wrap around his neck, holding him tight as we kiss like we'll never need to come up for air until he breaks away in a brusk movement.

"Wh—"

"Fuck, baby, you're too goddamn tempting," he groans, thrusting his hips to rub against my now slick heat. "No more kissing."

"B-but you kissed me!" I whine, not sure if I'm more annoyed he stopped kissing or that he's trying to blame me for our current predicament.

"Because you're too fucking gorgeous," he growls, shaking his head and forcing out a deep breath. "Right, I'm the Dom here. I can control myself," he chastises himself, making me giggle. "Oh, you think that's funny, do you?"

"Uh-huh," I tease until his hands move to my sides, tickling me. "No! No, fuck!" I cry out, thrashing around. I fucking hate being tickled to my very core.

"You want to laugh at my struggles, little miss?" he teases, tickle attacking me until I'm falling off of his lap and onto the couch, gasping for breath. I'm fighting for my damn life as he continues to attack me, kicking and flailing like I'm in a battle.

Fuck, I really do hate being tickled.

"Oof," I hear Dameon grunt, and he stops tickling me. "Christ," he groans, and I sit up fast as realization dawns on me.

"Oh no," I whisper. "D? Ah, shit," I curse, and he grunts.

"Stop swearing in little space," he pushes through clenched teeth.

"Are you seriously giving me crap right now? I just kicked you in the dick!" Has he lost his mind? If there's something to knock me back into big headspace, it's making out with a hot guy then kicking him in the jewels. "I kicked you in the junk. Crap! Are you okay? Do you need ice or something?" I ask, firing questions faster than he has the ability to answer.

"Abbs, shh," he reaches one arm out to grab hold of me while the other continues to cup his dick. "Chill out."

Right. I'll get right on that.

## CHAPTER 31
## DAMEON

Fuck, that hurt. I haven't felt a shot to the balls since high school, and I think it hurts worse now than it did when I was younger, Jesus Christ.

"Abbs, chill," I tell her again after taking a deep breath.

"I can't just chill, Dameon!" she snaps, but I let it slide.

"Did you kick me in the dick on purpose?" I ask as I sit up straight, the pain slowly dulling. It definitely took the erection away, so that shot was probably a blessing in disguise.

Abby has the ability to make me forget to be reasonable, apparently, but fuck, she tastes delicious.

"What? No! That's just mean." She frowns and I

can't help but smile at how cute she is. Before she panicked over my slip up, her little was coming out full force and she was so damn cute.

"Then it's fine. Look, I'm fine." I stare her down until her shoulders relax. "But I will remember that tickling is a hard limit," I promise, making her snort.

"Good. I really am sorry, though. Your poor dilly-willy. I'm sorry, little dude," she talks to my dick.

"Hey, now, he isn't small. You're going to give him a complex," I argue without thinking. What the fuck? Where did that come from? Maybe there's more of a daddy in me than I thought. "And you aren't calling him dilly-willy."

"But it's cute," Abby says, looking at me with puppy dog eyes that sparkle with mischief.

"Enough of that, brat," I tell her, making her laugh.

"Sheesh, so sensitive. I think maybe you're the one with a complex, D," she sasses.

"Har-har, Abbs." Shaking my head, I can't help but smile at her. I love seeing her like this. "Okay, now that I can breathe again, let's get back to the conversation we're dancing around."

She closes her eyes, taking a deep breath and nodding her head. "Yeah, I guess it's kind of an important convo to have, huh?"

"It is," I agree, watching her. "You were having fun until I mentioned punishment. Is that what sent you into a panic? You thought I would hurt you?" I force my voice to remain calm, but a deeper part of me is seething.

Not for the first time, I find myself frustrated and angry at just how misrepresented sadism is in the world. Even those in the kink lifestyle can misconstrue the true feelings and dynamic behind it if they aren't a part of it or willing to do their research.

"D," Abigail starts, "I don't think you hurt them on purpose. At least, not without their consent. I just... I can't, D. I really can't." Her voice breaks as her hands shake, and it hurts me to see her feel this afraid.

"Hey, it's good to know your limits, sweetness. Why are you getting so upset?" I have a fair idea of why, given her statement about not being what I need, but a huge part of any D/s dynamic is being open about everything. I need her to voice her fears and concerns so we can battle them together.

"Because... because I can't give you what you need, Dameon. Why are you making this so much harder?" she asks gently, and I pull her close to me and grip her chin.

"Abigail, I need you to put your listening ears on

right now, okay?" I ask, and she frowns. "You have a tendency to be stubborn as fuck and not listen once you've set your mind on something, baby, and this is really important."

"Okay." She swallows. "Okay, I'm listening."

"Good girl." Leaning down, I kiss her forehead before pulling back. "Being a sadist isn't all about using instruments and causing physical pain. I don't necessarily get off on causing the pain, I get off on the power it gives me when my partner thrives off it."

I can see the confusion on her face. It's not that she isn't hearing me, but she's having a hard time connecting what I'm saying to what she's heard or read about.

"But—"

"No buts. I don't need to cause physical pain. Each and every dynamic is different and negotiated. If it's not something my partner is into, it does nothing for me, and I would never push someone's hard limits," I explain.

"I hear what you're saying, but I'm not grasping it. You identify as a sadist, right?"

I smirk. "I do. But if you think spanking, flogging, and any type of impact play is the only form of pain and punishment I can give you, then I'm going to greatly enjoy proving you wrong, sweetness." I'm getting hard just thinking about all of the ways to cause her pleasurable pain.

"I don't want you to try and be something you're not," she whispers, averting her eyes.

Gripping her chin tighter, I pull her face closer to mine, forcing her to see only me. "You aren't, Abbs. I promise you, you aren't. Everyone has their limits, sweetness, and it's perfectly okay."

"Are you—are we doing this? You want me to be your submissive?" she asks, her voice shaky.

"I do. I want you to be my submissive, my little girl, my woman. I want you to be fucking mine, Abigail. What do you say, baby? You want to go on this adventure with me?"

Her eyes bore into mine, searching for any sort of hesitation, but she won't find it. I've been lying to myself for weeks now, maybe even longer when it comes to this girl. And yeah, that makes me feel like a creep, but I never actually *saw* her as anything other than a pain in my ass until I was forced to see a life where she possibly wouldn't exist.

There's a reason this girl gets under my skin and always has, and it's because she was fucking made for me just as I was made to protect her.

"Yeah. Yeah, I really do." She smiles with tears in her eyes. "I'm insane to agree to this when you get on my nerves more than anyone else on the entire damn planet, but..." she trails off.

"But?" I ask, running my nose along hers.

"But you're the only person who has ever made me feel safe. Maybe this will all come crashing down some day, but I don't care. I need to at least try."

I growl, kissing her hard and fast before pulling away. "It won't come crashing down, Abigail. I won't let anything ever hurt you. Including me."

It's a vow I will take to the fucking grave. If anyone tries to hurt her in any way, I'll bury them.

# CHAPTER 32
# ABIGAIL

RULES, SAFE WORDS, LIMITS. AND HOMEWORK. I thought I was finished with homework for a while, but apparently not.

"Did you get that list finished, Abbs?" D asks when we're done having dinner.

He joined me on my call with Derek, and we all talked about entering this type of dynamic after everything I've been through. Derek suggested to take it slow, but he knows it can be healing to some like it was for Lana. And that Dameon taking on a daddy role may just help me start to replace the really shitty memories I have with my own in a sense.

"Yeah, I think so. I can adjust it at any point, right?" I ask, not for the first time since we started this talk earlier. You know, after D recovered from my kick to the nuts.

"Always. Your limits can fluctuate and flow all of the time. Some things may become hard limits that you haven't even thought about right now, while others could end up being removed. It's not set in stone, and it's all under your control, sweetness." Damn, he's so fucking sexy when he's caring and attentive like this.

Okay, fine. He's sexy all of the time, but I don't feel the urge to punch him when he's sweet.

"Then yeah, I'm good," I tell him, pulling the folded up paper from my pocket and handing it to him.

It's a standard list of hard limits from what I can see online, and honestly, some of them shocked me as being a fetish or kink. Not that I'm shaming anyone, but it definitely proves I know next to nothing about this lifestyle and community.

The list I created for D to read looks just like this:

## HARD LIMITS
- CHOKING
- IMPACT PLAY

- FECAL OR URINE PLAY

- KNIFE AND BLOOD PLAY

- DADDY/DAUGHTER ROLE PLAY (WHICH I'VE LEARNED IS SO GREATLY DIFFERENT THAN DDLG. I HAD TO ASK LANA ABOUT THAT ONE. SORRY FOR THE INFO, DUDE HAHAHA). —TO EACH THEIR OWN, IT'S JUST NOT REALLY MY THING.

- FISTING (JUST THE THOUGHT OF IT MAKES ME WINCE. PROPS TO THE BABES AND DUDES THAT CAN DO THIS, THOUGH. I'D LOVE TO WATCH IT GO DOWN AT SOME POINT.)

- HUMILIATION

- CAGES (I'VE FELT LOCKED AWAY TOO LONG ALREADY, D.)

## SOFT LIMITS

- DEGRADATION (NEEDS TO BE MIXED WITH PRAISE OR IT'S TOO CLOSE TO WHAT HE DID TO ME. MAY NEED TO MOVE TO HARD LIMITS, BUT I WANT TO TRY FIRST.)

- ANAL (I KNOW WE DISCUSSED PLUGS FOR PUNISHMENT, I'M JUST NOT SURE THAT MONSTER OF YOURS WILL EVER FIT IN MY ASS, DUDE.)

## SAFE WORD:

TECHNO (I HATE IT. TRUST ME, I WILL NEVER SAY
THIS DURING PUNISHMENT OR SEXY TIMES)

## NON-VERBAL CUES:

DOUBLE TAP WITH A PINCH.

Dameon laughs and shakes his head as he reads through my jokes, making my heart flutter. Damn, when did he turn me into such a sap? Sheesh, I'm a regular swoon girl from rom-coms right now.

*Ah hell, I'm Rose.*

"This is great, Abigail. I'm fucking proud of you, baby." He stands up and walks over to me, pulling me into his arms and kissing my head. "I promise I will adhere to everything you've ever put on there, but I'll do you one better."

I look up at him in confusion and he smiles at me softly, running his hand down my hair.

"If you say no as well, I will stop and check in with you to make sure you're not just too over-whelmed to remember your safe-word, okay?" he promises, and my eyes well up with tears.

Fucking hell, I've never been this emotional in my life. Maybe my period is coming. "Yeah, D, that sounds perfect," I rasp, standing on my toes to kiss him gently on the lips.

I can't believe this man is all mine.

Stupid. How is it that I sleep in the man's arms for one night and suddenly I can't sleep on my own? Honestly, it's bullshit.

Huffing a breath, I throw the blanket off of me and start pacing the floor.

"Dammit, Abby, get your shit together. Just because he's your Dom now doesn't mean you can just expect him to fuck you because you're horny," I say, chastising myself.

But I am horny. I have been for weeks at this point, and when I tried to take care of that problem last night, I woke the entire damn ranch up. Mind you, it ended with Dameon claiming me, so I can't exactly complain.

Fuck it. Getting up, I stomp to the door and swing it open, running right into a hard chest. "Ooomph."

"Going somewhere, sweetness?" D purrs above, and my cheeks heat. Shit, this man has me all twisted up.

"Yep! Thirsty," I squeak, groaning when he chuckles.

"Hmm, thirsty could be taken a lot of ways, baby. What were you thirsty for?" He leans down, whispering into my ear, sending a shiver down my spine.

"Uh..." Can I tell him the truth?

"No lies, Abigail. Tell me what you want," he whispers, nipping my ear with his teeth, and I snap.

I pull back, wrapping my hands around his neck and bringing his mouth to mine to kiss him with everything I have. All of the desire and passion I feel for this man, poured into one intense kiss.

"You. I'm thirsty for you, D," I growl and bite his lip.

"Fuck yeah, baby." He grabs my ass and lifts me up, wrapping my legs around him while he kisses me hard. "Good girl for telling me the truth," D praises, and I melt into him.

I'm aware he's moving us away from my room, and for a moment I worry he's going to cut this short until my back is pushed against the doorframe to his bedroom.

"What?" I ask, wondering why we couldn't just do this where we were, but he just smirks at me.

"I have a king-sized bed, Abbs, and I want to have enough room to explore every goddamn inch of you while we're both comfortable." He kisses me hard. "And your room is the place you have that's yours, baby. I want it to stay your safe space, but don't think I'm not moving you to my bed, baby. Because from here on out, you sleep where I sleep. You. Are. Mine. Get me?" he growls, and I whimper and grind against his hardening cock.

"I get you. Now please, Dameon, fuck me."

## CHAPTER 33
## DAMEON

Oh, she wants to get sassy right now? Two can play at that game.

"Poor baby." I shake my head. "Do you need to be fucked?"

"You know I do," she snarls, making me smirk.

"Is that how you ask your Dom to please you?" I question, grinding my cock against her sweet cunt.

The whimper-moan she makes goes straight to the needy bastard. I'm not sure I've ever been this hard in my fucking life and I've barely done shit.

"Urgh! D, please. Please make me cum," she begs so sweetly, and I kiss her hungrily walking us over to the bed.

"Good girl, but you can do better than that."

The fire inside her ignites, and I know she's

about to make this so much fun for me. I think I'm already in love with her, for fuck's sake.

Watching Abigail climb onto her knees on the bed and slowly stripping off her shirt is enough to have my cock aching, forcing me to squeeze it through my boxers. "Christ," I hiss out.

"Will you please do me the honour of fucking me senseless... Sir?" she purrs while undoing her bra, and I'm on her before she can blink.

"Mine," I growl, forcing her hands into one of mine, bringing them to her lower back. "Mmm, naughty girl. You shouldn't be stripping without Sir's permission, but I'll let it slide. Kind of," I taunt, kissing her again as I slide her bra down her arms and making quick work of tying her hands behind her.

Its not tight enough to harm her, and she can easily get free if needed, but it will be a reminder for her to keep her hands where they belong. "Don't move those hands until I tell you to, Abbs. Understood?"

"Yes, Sir," she breathes out, and I smile.

"Good girl for addressing me that way, baby." I kiss her gently and move her to kneel in the centre of the bed. "How about I'm Sir in the bedroom and then Daddy out there when you're ready?"

She hasn't called me daddy today, but I also know it's going to be hard for her to let those walls down, and I don't mind. The fact that she's acknowledging my dominance over her in other ways is enough for me. We do this at her pace.

"That works for me," Abby moans out as I kiss her neck.

"Sir."

"Crap. Uh, that works for me, Sir," she corrects, and I growl, biting down softly on her neck.

"Good fucking girl." I kiss her neck once more then move back to her mouth, pushing my tongue against hers and swallowing her moans.

Pulling away, my cock throbs between us as I squeeze it tightly, choking the bastard. He knows exactly what we're about to do and wants to be a part of the party, but he'll have to wait.

"Abbs, sweetness, if you want anything to stop at any time, what's your safeword?"

"Techno," she breathes out, and I nod.

"Good girl. Say it and everything stops so I can check in with you, okay?"

"Yes. Sir," she corrects at the last second, making me smile.

"Good. Now buckle up, baby. You're about to go for a ride."

She stares at me in confusion before her eyes widen when I lay on my back before her. "Oh shit."

"Don't worry, baby. I'll hold you up, but you're cumming at least twice on my tongue before you get this cock. Now, turn around and don't forget to keep those hands where they are," I warn her, relishing in the shiver that runs through her at my dominance.

The second she's turned around, I bite my lip and stare up at her delectable ass. God, I'd love to take a bite out of it just to hear her squeal for me.

"Spread your knees, baby."

"Yes, Sir," she breathes out, following my direction so beautifully.

"Fuck, baby, you're perfect." Praising Abigail is as easy as fucking breathing, and the fact she flourishes under it just makes it that much easier.

Sliding between her legs, the scent of her arousal has my mouth watering, and I'm ready to devour my woman entirely until she can't remember her own name. But I want to tease her, and make her feel so fucking good first. This isn't a race, and there's no real skill in getting her off as fast as possible.

I'm going to make sure she forgets whatever little shits she's allowed to fuck her before me. She's mine now and forever, and she's about to know it.

"I hope these aren't your favourite," I say as I rip

the thong off her, making sure she feels the sting of the fabric cutting into her hips before it breaks.

"Christ," she hisses, moaning when my nose rubs against her clit.

"Mmm, you're so wet for me, sweetness. You want me to lick this sweet cunt until you cream for me?"

"Yes. Please, fuck yes." She lowers herself to grind against my face, making me chuckle and grip her ass cheeks in my hands.

Flicking my tongue out, I tease her slickness with the tip, slowly parting her lips as I go. "God, baby. You taste delicious," I growl against her, repeating the movements while squeezing her ass.

"Sir, please," she whines when I notch my tongue inside her entrance. She's already so close as I fuck her with the tip my tongue, I know teasing her is going to be brutal. She's shaking with need so much already, I'm not sure she'll be able to hold off on an orgasm either.

Poor baby.

"That's it, sweetness. Fucking smother me, baby." I pull her ass down so she's grinding my face hard as I move her back and forth on my tongue, sliding it into her entrance every chance I get before moving the attention back to her clit.

"Fuck, fuck, fuck," she cries out, grinding down harder. "Yes, Daddy!" she screams as she cums all over my face, grinding and crying out as she shatters. And fuck me if my balls don't draw up, ready to shoot their load before we've even felt her.

## CHAPTER 34
## ABIGAIL

HOLY MOTHER OF FUCKING HELL! THAT WAS THE BEST orgasm of my goddamn life, and I want more.

"Mmmmm," D groans against my clit, sending aftershocks through me as I try to catch my breath.

"Fucking hell, D," I moan, circling my hips and shrieking when he pinches my ass. "Sir!" I correct breathlessly.

He chuckles under me before doubling down his efforts again, stoking the fires of desire in me until I'm once again finding it hard to breathe and focus.

I should be worried about the fact that I called him Daddy when I came, but he's making me feel too good to care right now. Every stroke of his tongue through my folds sends me crashing toward the edge of that cliff once again.

I know he said I had to cum more than once before he took me, but I honestly thought multiple orgasms were a myth and he'd get bored. Clearly, I was the one in the wrong because the moment he sucks my clit between his teeth, I'm crashing through another orgasm, screaming my release.

"Sir! Fuck, yesssss!" I cry and scream, shaking as I collapse forward while I tremble through the orgasm he's wrung from me.

Without waiting, D releases my arms and rolls us over, sliding his hard body between my thighs and kissing me hard, forcing me to taste myself.

"Fuck, Abbs, you're so goddamn stunning, baby," he praises me before kissing me softly again, making me blush.

"I called you... uh, you know," I state, waving my hands around before covering my face.

His chuckle is adorable as he reaches between us to pull my hands away. "No hiding from me, Abigail." It's a stern order that has me dropping my hands through my embarrassment.

"Sorry, D," I whisper, and he quirks a brow.

"I'll let that slide since we're having a serious conversation, even if we are naked and I'm about to fuck you like your life depends on it."

I bark out a laugh and his smile grows.

"You did that on purpose, huh?" I ask, and he nods.

"You bet. You have no reason to ever be embarrassed, Abigail. Not with me."

"I called you Daddy when I came, D. That's weird!"

"Is it? I think it was bound to happen because you want to call me Daddy, you just can't let your guard down easily. When you're mid orgasm, you're at your most vulnerable. You let your walls drop, Abigail, and that's okay. Besides, I almost nutted in my boxers when you screamed it." The red cheeks he's sporting makes my head spin. He can be so cute sometimes. A royal pain in my ass, but definitely cute.

"Speaking of boxers..." I reach behind him and start pushing them down his ass. "You are far too clothed now that you have me naked, Sir." Using the bedroom honourifics seems to do the trick, and he takes the out I'm giving him easily, shedding the boxers until there's nothing between us.

Sometimes it's scary how well D can read me with ease, but I guess it's just the connection we share. Or a part of how observant he is as a whole, but probably a mixture of a lot of things. Whatever the cause, I'm grateful. He's been able to stop me from spiralling into another self-harming episode, and that's a big deal.

"Damn, Abbs, if you wanted to see my dick all you had to do was ask," he smarts off with a smirk, making me giggle. The humour is replaced by hunger the second my eyes land on the cock in question pointing right at me.

When Dameon strokes himself, moaning, I cant help but feel myself get impossibly wetter. I don't know why it's so hot to watch him handle his own dick, but I freaking love it.

"God, baby, don't look at me like that," he groans and climbs onto the bed, once again sliding between my legs to hover over me.

"Like what?" I swallow, feeling nervous about taking this step with D. It's not that I don't want him, but what if I can't measure up to the other women he's been with?

"Like you're dying to suck my cock between those beautiful, pouty lips of yours," he says, kissing me passionately as his hand moves into my hair and tugs hard. "I don't need you to tell me whatever the self deprecating thought was that just flashed through your head a moment ago, Abbs, but you better cut that shit out."

"I—" What the hell do I say to that?

"No, Abigail. You feel this?" He grinds his hardness into my thigh, making me whimper. When I nod yes, his hold on my hair tightens even more. "That's for you, sweetness. God, baby, I have never been this turned on in my fucking life, so whatever was going through your mind? Let it go, because I promise you here and now that it was complete and utter bullshit."

And I believe him when he looks at me like this. "Yes, Sir," I whisper, meaning every word.

"Good girl." D kisses me with a gentleness I've never seen from him, but it quickly becomes heated when his tongue starts tangling with mine. "Fuck, baby."

"I'm yours, D," I whisper, needing to make sure he knows I mean as more than his submissive. That even outside of this bedroom, I'm his woman, his partner, his equal. Not just his submissive little. "Make me yours, Sir."

A fire blazes in his eyes as he reaches between us and grips his cock, moving to slide the head through my wet core. "You're still sure you don't want me to grab a condom? I don't want to put you at risk, sweetness."

I smile and wrap my arms around his neck while letting my legs do the same around his waist. "I have the arm implant. I told you, I'm good. Please, Sir, I don't want anything between us."

A moment passes between us as he looks into my eyes, stealing my breath. He leans down to kiss me and lines the head of his cock with my entrance then slowly starts sliding in, stretching me like never before.

"Oh," I moan into his mouth, tightening my hold on him as he continues to slide deeper into me.

"Fuck, baby," he groans. "You're so damn perfect." D comes to a stop when he's fully seated in my pussy, stretching and filling me to the very brim.

"I think I'm going to cum," I tell him truthfully, feeling overwhelmed and sensitive from the two previous orgasms he's given me already. "You're stretching me so good."

"And you're squeezing me so goddamn tight I'm going to embarrass myself with how quickly I cum, baby."

I giggle, making him arch a brow in challenge before he pulls back a few inches and slams forward, changing my giggle to a groan as I toss my head back. "Fuuckkkkk."

"That's it, sweetness. Take Sir's cock like a good girl," he tells me, pulling back until he's barely inside of me before pushing back in with one swift thrust.

"God, yes!" I cry out, loving how good he feels as he continues to fuck me with both gentleness and intensity, making me feel things I've never felt while fucking Ted or anyone else.

"Yeah, baby, there you go," he praises as he begins thrusting faster and harder, a sheen of sweat covering us both as we chase that euphoric release. "Cum for me, Abigail. Cum all over my cock like my perfect girl, baby."

"Daemon!" I scream his name as I cum, following his command as if my body isn't my own.

"Fucking hell," he curses, his hips losing rhythm as they grind against me. "Abigail, fuck!" I feel him jerk inside of me, his cum splashing against my walls and sending me into another tiny orgasm.

It feels so fucking good I never want to come down from the pleasure he's giving me right now, but I know it's not the last time. Not now, not ever.

"Mmm, that was... incredible," I yawn with a smile, still holding him inside of me as we come down from the high. I'm freaking wrecked in the best ways possible though, and I want to sleep so fucking bad.

"Mind-blowing, intense, incredible. Life changing," D says, kissing me softly. "It was everything, sweetness." He kisses me again as he slowly pulls out of me, and I whimper at the loss of contact. "Shhh, baby. I need to get a warm cloth to clean you up and then you can sleep, okay?"

"Mmmm otay, Daddy. Sleep sounds soooo good," I say sleepily, my eyes closed as I snuggle into his pillow.

I vaguely remember hearing him chuckle as he walks away before falling into a deep sleep.

## CHAPTER 35
## DAMEON

Waking up to Abigail beside me is the sweetest form of torture.

I thought waking up beside her when I held her the night before made me hard, but waking up and remembering how good she felt sheathing my cock? How mine she was? Well, that just about trumps anything else I have ever felt before in my life.

Quickly, I wrap the covers around her and move out of bed, trying not to wake her. Once I'm sure Abby isn't waking up, I move to the dresser and grab a fresh pair of boxers and jeans, tossing them on and snatching my phone to go make us some breakfast.

Abigail has been slowly getting to the point where she can stomach more than a smoothie for breakfast, and I'm so fucking proud of her for that. But I need to make sure she eats or she will just revert back to going all day without food.

Just as I'm about to put the garlic bread in the oven, my phone vibrates in my pocket. Cursing, I quickly slide the tray into the heated oven then grab my phone.

"Hey, Sheriff. To what do I owe this early morning call?" I greet Travis, but his silence is enough to have the smile dropping from my face.

"I wish it was some good news, man, but it's not. I was just notified this morning and called you first." Travis is a busy man, and even busier since he's had to take over the mayoral role for Abigail's father until the entire office is done being investigated and they find a new candidate.

"Tell me what? What's going on?" I plant my hands on the counter and lean forward with the phone between my shoulder and ear, bracing for whatever he's about to tell me.

"Davies was released on bail last night."

"He was WHAT?!" I shout, unable to contain my disbelief. "How the fuck did that happen? Where is the bastard right now, Travis?"

He sighs. "Ethan followed him out of town, but

you should know something, Dameon," he hedges. "Senator Boon is the one who bailed him out."

"Christ," I hiss, shaking my head as I start to pace the kitchen.

Boon has been someone we've had to keep an eye on ever since we found out Lana's abusive ex was his illegitimate son. When Travis killed him to save Lana, we knew there would most likely be retaliation of some kind, but it hadn't even occurred to me that Abigail's father could be friends with the prick.

"You're telling me," Travis groans. "Dameon, I don't think this was an accident or coincidence. It's well known that Abigail is under the protection of the Easton brothers and staying at Serenity," he warns, and I nod as Abigail's feet shuffle down the hall.

"No, I'd bet every last cent I have that there are no coincidences in this scenario," I agree with him as Abby rounds the corner, rendering me speechless in one of my shirts. "I gotta go, man. I'll talk to Abby after breakfast."

"Yeah, thanks. I'll try and swing by later this afternoon if I can."

"D?" Abigail asks when I hang up the phone.

"Morning, beautiful," I greet, reaching to pull her

into my arms for a deep and sensual kiss that leaves her breathless. I hate that I'm about to start our day off like this.

"Mmm, morning," she says, biting my lip and pulling back. "What's wrong? You just told someone you'd talk to me after breakfast."

"Mhm, I did, but it's not after breakfast. Eat first, then talk, Abbs. Can you do that for me?"

She eyes me suspiciously for a moment then nods. "Fine, but only because I smell garlic bread and that means it's scrambled eggs and fruit day, and I can tell what you're about to drop is gonna suck."

"You've already caught on to my culinary limitations, huh?" I wince, making her laugh.

"Yeah, Daddy, it wasn't that hard to figure out," she sasses in a slightly higher voice.

She blushes and ducks her head a bit, shy for calling me Daddy and trying to let her little out for the first time where we both know the score, and I can't have that.

"That's right, sweetness. I am the daddy, and you're my girl, so watch the sass, little miss." I boop her nose for good measure, and the startling giggle she lets out warms my chest more than I ever thought possible.

"Sorry, Daddy," she says coyly, and I smirk.

"Oh you look so repentant," I tell her cheekily before kissing the tip of her nose and pulling back. "Now go have a seat and wait for Daddy."

"Wait for you?" Abigail asks in confusion.

"Yes, little miss. Little girls can't be handling hot food." I point my spatula toward her. "They could get burned. Let me plate your food and make sure it's safe for you to eat it."

Damn, I don't know where any of this is coming from right now. It's not like I've ever really treated Lana this way or seen Trent do so. No, this is more how I imagine Carl would be with his forever little. It doesn't really matter though, because seeing her little peaking out is enough to settle everything inside of me.

We can talk about the other bastard when she's big again. For now, I just want her to be at peace, and being little is giving that to her.

**ABIGAIL**

"Hey, little miss, what are you drawing?" Daddy asks me when he comes back into the room.

I've been little for a couple of hours now, but I love it. I just want to bask in this relaxation before I get the news that made him all grumpy this morning, and I can tell he needs this too.

It was weird at first, letting my walls down to slip into little space, but it's honestly the bestest! And having Lana and Rina to talk to about it really helped me explore on my own before letting D in on it.

"Can't you tell, Daddy?" I ask him in the most childlike voice I've ever heard come from me. "You has to know whats it is, Daddy!"

"Hmm, let me get a closer look, baby," he says, playing along. There's absolutely no way he can tell what it is. Technically, it started as one thing and then I just felt like squiggles really needed to be all over the page, so you know.

"Okee, here." I pass him the paper and watch as he examines it.

"You know, little miss, I don't think I do." He tilts his head, making me giggle. "It sure is a masterpiece though. Can Daddy hang it up on the fridge? I just bet an art collector will want it some day," he says with all seriousness.

God, this is fun.

"You really think so, Daddy?" I gasp. "You won't

sell it though, rights? It's a Daddy Special." I give him a stern look, feeling so carefree and happy when he smiles.

"Never, baby. It's far too special to let anyone else get their grimy paws all over it," he says, leaning down to kiss me on the forehead. "Come on, little miss. It's lunch time."

Ewww, no food. "I don't wanna. I'm colouring!" I whine, partially surprising myself.

"Hmm, sounds like someone is in need of some corner time and a nap."

Ah, tootlefudgesticks. "Nope! I good girl, Daddy. Lunch? Nummmm." I rub my belly and jump up, making him laugh.

"That's what I thought. Come on, baby. We'll have lunch and see where we're at, okay?" he says, taking my hand and guiding me into the kitchen.

Taking a deep breath, I close my eyes and nod while squeezing his hand in mine.

"Okay, Daddy. I can be big after lunch though, okay? I just—"

"I know, sweetness. Hey, look at me," he says, tilting my face to look him in the eyes. "I've loved seeing your little and being called Daddy. I wouldn't trade this morning for freaking anything, Abbs. You take as long as you need, okay?"

"You're the best, Daddy."

"Aww, thanks, baby. I'm trying. Now, lunch. I'm a very hungry Daddy."

Giggling, I move to the table and sit down, waiting for D to join me before digging in.

## CHAPTER 36
## ABIGAIL

"Hey, babe," Rose says through the phone the second she picks up.

"Rose, he got bail and disappeared," I rush in a panic.

It's been an hour since D told me that my father was released on bail and left town, but I don't think he'll cower away so easily. I know him and he isn't the backing down type.

No, he will come back and finish what he started that night because he'll blame me for losing everything. Just like he always has.

"Oh fuck!" my bestie curses, making me shake my head. I'll never get used to her swearing. "What do you want to do, babe?"

Run. It's the only thing I can think of because I

can't hide here forever. He'll get to me one way or another, but I can run and save everyone else.

"Don't even say it, Abigail Davies. I will spank your ass if you say it," Rose hisses down the line, making me cackle despite how I'm feeling.

The urge to cut is so strong right now it's practically suffocating me.

"I'd love to see you try, Rosie."

"I swear to fuck, I'm going to kill your father myself." Rose blows out a breath. "You're safe there, babe. Dameon would never let anything happen to you."

"I know, but I don't want to risk anyone getting hurt. Fuck, Rose, Lana has been through enough already without my father being a threat."

"Babe, you tried to break out to get laid and set off enough security it made the White House look like McDonalds. You're both safer there than anywhere else."

"So, what? I just hide here forever and never leave the house?" I huff down the line.

"No, you just make sure that sexy man of yours is with you when you do leave. They'll catch him if he comes near you, babe. Have faith."

Maybe she's right. Maybe I won't be putting them in danger. But what if I am? I'd never forgive myself if something bad happened to any of them because of me.

No. It's better for me to try and find a way out of here, I just have to wait for the right time. Like the day I write my final exam.

"You're right," I tell her, a lead ball sinking in my tummy for leading her on.

"Uh huh, you're damn right I am! Now go cuddle that sexy man of yours and have hot sex like in your books so you can tell me all about it."

"ROSE!" I screech, my cheeks heating beyond belief as she cackles down the line.

"Love you! Now relax and have fun."

"Love you too, you psycho," I mutter with a smile before hanging up the phone after saying goodbye.

"Abbs, you okay?" D asks through the door, no doubt worried from my squeal.

"I'm good. I was just talking to Rose," I tell him, opening the door to stare up at his handsome face. A face I rode hard last night. I think I'd love a repeat of just that right now.

"I can see your wheels spinning," he says quietly, tapping the side of my head with his finger. "You've been struggling and I'm worried."

I know what he's worried about, and truthfully, so am I. God, I want to relapse so badly but I can't. I won't. Not over that son of a bitch. He's hurt me enough.

"So am I," I admit, earning me a gentle kiss. "D, I don't feel right."

"I know, sweetness. I can see that. Do you want to get into some comfy jammies and watch a movie together?" he asks, squeezing me tight.

"I don't know that I can go little right now."

"I didn't say you had to. We'll watch whatever you want to watch, I just want to hold you. You're not alone, Abigail. I'm right here and I won't let you fall. Even when you feel like you're drowning."

"How can you be so perfect?" I whisper against his chest as tears burn my eyes.

D snorts and pulls back, resting his hands on my shoulders. "I'm not perfect, Abbs, I'm just perfect for you." He winks and gives me a cocky smile, lightening the mood just a little, and I think I love him for it.

Oof, now that's a big feeling I can't process right now. So, distraction it is. "Any movie?" I ask, feeling sassy all of a sudden.

"Any movie. So, what form of torture will it be, m'lady?" D asks with a horrible accent as he takes a bow.

I can't help the laughter that escapes me when

he looks up mid bow and waggles his eyebrows suggestively.

"Wow, that was a terrible accent. Never do that again," I say, still laughing.

D stands and shrugs, pulling me back into his arms and kissing the tip of my nose. "It got you to laugh, Abbs. That's all I care about."

Damn, this man.

"Fine, let me get dressed and I'll meet you out there." I push him away with a smile.

"What kind of snacks does my girl want?" he asks, his face looking deadly serious.

"Why? Is this a quiz?"

"Damn right it is, baby. If you say something like fresh fruit salad, that's in direct violation of movie night rules." His tone says he's serious but the twitch of his mouth betrays him, making me smile.

"Good thing I happen to agree with said etiquette. For movie nights at least. Now, midday movies is another story completely," I tease, and he gives me a sharp nod.

"We're on the same page then. Good." He's starting to smile and it warms my anxiety the more I see it.

"Popcorn and meat sticks?" I question with a raised eyebrow.

D clutches his chest and gasps. "Fuck yes! A woman after my own heart. On it."

I laugh as he walks away before closing the door and looking around the quiet room. Now that he's left me alone again, I can feel the anxiety and worry creeping back in, and my fingers twitch, needing to hold that blade between my fingers. To take the control back in my life that my father so easily took from me.

I need to feel like I can fucking breathe again, and that's the only way I know how. I need to feel that blade cut into my skin and watch the blood drip out, letting the emotions flow from me in a way that keeps me under control. But I can't. I don't need to do that anymore when I have Dameon supporting me, keeping me safe.

"Hey, D?" I holler through the door, quickly changing into a thick sweater and yoga pants.

"Yeah, sweetness?" he asks, his voice travelling down the hall along with his footsteps.

When he reaches my door, I turn to look at him. Once our eyes connect, I take the first steadying breath I can since he left me a few moments earlier.

Squaring my shoulders, I tell him the truth.

"I'm not okay, Dameon. I need to not be left

alone for a bit," I whisper, and he nods in understanding while walking over to me.

"Then I'll be right by your side every step of the way, Abbs. I'm right here."

God, I don't know how I got lucky enough to fall for my sworn annoyance, but I'm so grateful I did.

## CHAPTER 37
## DAMEON

ROSE:

Be warned. I think Abby is going to try and run.

THAT'S THE TEXT ROSE SENT ME THREE DAYS AGO, AND I've been on edge ever since.

I knew there was a chance she'd run from fear, not that she'd get far. No, she's my woman. Mine to protect, to love, and to punish for trying to put her ass in danger which is exactly what running will do.

Mine and Rose's suspicions were confirmed when I noticed her going to spend more time with Star than normal, always leaving with something seemingly small and insignificant but not bringing it back.

It doesn't take a rocket scientist to figure out that she's trying to stock up on just what she needs before running. Thing is, I don't think she actually wants to run, she just feels like it's her only option. Just like Lana did when she ran from us and almost got herself killed.

Fucking hell, the women in my life are trying to kill me.

"You okay, man?" Travis asks while he, Trent, and I watch the girls playing.

Seeing Abigail be little and carefree has been an experience that I'd never trade for anything, but it's fairly obvious she's fighting her little pretty hard right now. To me, anyway.

"I'm good. I think she's going to attempt to run today," I explain, and they both look at me.

"You sure?" Trent questions, his face darkening as he thinks of the night Lana ran from us. It damn near killed us all when we woke up to her gone.

"Positive." I nod, turning away from the girls while keeping them in my peripheral vision. She won't make a move if she thinks I'm staring her down, and I need her to. I need her to try and run so I can prove to her she's safe with me.

"Fuck. Why today?" Travis asks on a low breath.

"Just a feeling. I think she was going to wait until tomorrow, but she's antsy as fuck. I don't think she has the ability to sit on it any longer."

"Tomorrow? When she writes her exam?" Trent asks.

"It's when I would try and run. She'll be away from the ranch and all of its security. If I were trying to run from something, the less security the better, right?" I shrug.

"You think she wants to get caught," Travis surmises, and I smirk.

"I think she wants to get caught, she just doesn't know it. She's terrified. Look at her." I nod in the direction where the girls are playing with beach toys in Lana's sandbox. Trent spoils my little sister way too fucking much, but Lord help me, I think I'll be the same way with Abigail.

"She looks kind of out of it," Trent says, and I agree.

"She's fighting her little really hard right now. I fucking hate that this bastard is upsetting her like this. Again," I growl, wishing I could strangle him with my bare hands.

"We'll figure it out, man. You need to breathe though. You're no good to her if you can't get it together," Trent tells me softly, and I take a deep breath, blowing it out just as Abby seems to excuse herself from the group.

"You're right. But I think she's on the move. I'll talk to you guys later."

"Sure, but bring her back. Once you've talked to her, I mean. I think she could use some little space once you've shown her she's safe," Travis supplies.

"Yeah, without a doubt. I'll see what I can do."

Turning away from them, I take the long way around to the barn where I know she'll be. I don't want her to hear me coming or see me, on the off chance she's being hyper aware right now.

When I reach the barn doors, I stop and listen, unable to stop the smile on my lips at what I hear.

"Don't look at me like that, Star," Abigail scolds my horse, her little definitely shining through now that she's alone. "No. Everything will be fine. You're such a good girl, aren't you, Star baby?"

Star whinnies and I look around the corner to see what's going on. She's looking at my woman like she's insane as Abby tries to lift the saddle onto her, failing miserably.

"Star, be nice. We're just going to go for a little ride, okay?"

When she falls on her ass, I decide enough is

enough and walk over to Star's stall. Abigail is too caught up in her little pout to notice my approach, but poor Star looks relieved to see me.

"A ride, huh?" I insert steel into my voice, making my little girl jump with a squeal. "Correct me if I'm wrong, little miss, but I'm fairly certain you haven't gotten up on a horse yet." I pin her with a look, and she blinks up at me as I join them in the stall.

"D, shit! You nearly gave me a heart attack!" she squeaks, her hand over her chest.

"I'll let the swearing slide since you're already in enough hot water, but don't think Daddy will let you swear at him in the future." I raise an eyebrow, watching her closely as she swallows her nervousness. "As for the scaring you part, if you weren't trying to run, you wouldn't have anything to fear, now would you?"

"Logic is dumb," she mumbles under her breath, deflating against the wall.

"Mmm, only to littles who don't tell their daddies what's bothering them," I counter, crouching down in front of her. "Talk to me, baby."

"Daddy," Abigail says, her bottom lip trembling. "I can't." She bursts into tears, my strong girl giving way to the little girl who has been scared for far too long.

"Shhh come here, sweetness." I fall to the ground and pull her into my lap, rocking her gently as she sobs in my arms. "I've got you. Daddy's got you, baby."

"I—I can't," she cries, burrowing deep into my chest as her body shakes. It breaks my fucking heart to see her like this.

"Shhh, let it all out, baby. I've got you," I whisper, running my hand down her back and holding her close.

"He—he's going to hurt you!" she cries harder, and I have to close my eyes and take a deep breath so she doesn't feel the anger inside of me and worry it's directed at her.

"He won't, sweetness. He can't touch me or you, I fucking promise."

She snorts through her tears. "So you can swear but I can't?" she sasses, easing the anger inside of me. She loves to have this slight disagreement in little space.

"You can swear, just not *at* me, little miss." I continue holding her close as she comes down from her upset until she pulls back to look up at me with a tear-stained face.

"I sowwy I swore at you, Daddy," she admits, wiping the snot on her nose with her sweater sleeve.

God, she's cute, but that definitely needs to go in the wash.

"You were scared. Are scared, so it's okay. I don't think you actually meant to curse at me, but we need to talk," I tell her gently, and she sighs big and loud.

"I know. I just... he's my worst nightmare, Daddy."

"Oh, sweetness. He may be your worst nightmare, but we're about to become his. He will never touch you again, understand?"

She swallows, looking up at me with big wide eyes, and nods. "Yes, Daddy."

"Good girl. Now, I have something for you. Travis actually just gave it to me when he arrived. Would my girl like to know what it is?"

She eyes me suspiciously. "I get a gift rather than a punishment?"

A dark laugh escapes me as I kiss her nose. "Oh, little miss, not even close. But this gift is also for your safety. I need you to promise never to take it off, alright?"

"My safety?" Abby asks in confusion.

Sliding her to my left thigh, I reach into my jean pocket and pull out the pouch that Travis handed me earlier. After we found out that Senator Boon was possibly involved, we put a rush order on some S.O.S bracelets for each of the girls.

"Yes, sweetness, your safety." I right her on my lap again before opening the pouch. "Trent, Travis, and myself all had these made for our girls." I kiss her gently.

"Oh my God, it's gorgeous!" she gasps, tears rimming her red eyes.

"Glad you think so, sweetness," I tell her as I clasp it onto her wrist. It dawns on me while doing it up that I would love to collar Abigail when she's ready for it because I know she's my forever. I can feel it in my fucking bones. "I love you, Abigail."

Her head flies up and her breath catches as she searches my face for something before she throws her arms around me. She kisses me hard as my hands move to the back of her head, taking control of the kiss as I pull her hair and push my tongue into her mouth.

Our tongues dance together as she holds onto me with a grip that conveys how much she owns me, and fuck if I don't love that.

"I love you too, Dameon. God, do I fucking love you, you royal pain in my ass," she sasses, making me laugh as my heart grows inside my chest.

"Such a sassy little brat," I tease, kissing her again. "I love you," I whisper against her lips.

"Love you too, Daddy. Now hurry up and tell me how this gorgeous bracelet is for my safety so you can fuck me."

Yeah, she was fucking made for me.

"Hmm, as much as I love that thought, there is the topic of punishment, which we will save for another day." I squeeze the back of her neck when I feel her tense up. "I don't want you to associate my telling you I love you with danger and punishment."

"O—kay?"

"I'll gladly claim you later on tonight, sweetness, I promise. However, we have company right now so stealing you away for sexy fun would be very naughty of us." I smirk, and she giggles.

"Yes, very naughty indeed. I can wait."

"Good girl." I kiss her head. "See this dial here?" I point to the side of the green pendant. "If you hold it down for three seconds, it sends an S.O.S to my phone and Travis'."

"Whoa, really?" Abigail stares at it in wonder.

"Yes really. If you're in danger or even just scared, don't hesitate to press that switch, Abigail. If it even crosses your mind to use it, fucking use it, you hear me?" I order, demanding she pays attention and listens to me.

"Yes, Daddy. I promise."

I nod. "Good girl. Come on, baby. Let's go play. I think my little miss needs some time to relax after big Abby fought her so long today."

"Yes please, Daddy."

# CHAPTER 38
# ABIGAIL

"WHOA, THAT'S A SUPER COOL BRACELET, ABBY!" RINA praises when I join them in the sandbox again.

Seriously. Lana has a freaking adult-sized sandbox because Trent is such a swoony dude for her. Totes head over heels for my girl.

"Thanks!" I beam, feeling myself slip into little space with ease now that I'm not fighting to run.

I never wanted to run in the first place, not really, but I didn't want to put any of them at risk. Truthfully, I was going through the motions. If I had really wanted to leave, I would have waited until I write my exam in two days. But I didn't. I chose to try and run in a reckless fashion, guaranteeing Daddy would catch me.

Also, I have no clue how to ride a horse, and Star

was being super less than helpful. So rude. I thought we were becoming besties.

"Oooo that means they're in?!" Lana squeals, clapping her hands. "Daddy totally showed me what he was getting. I'm excited!"

"Hey, you gets one too?" Rina whines, looking so darn cute.

"You do too, Pixie girl," Travis says, making me jump a little.

"I do?" Rina looks up at him with big eyes.

"Yes, baby. They're special S.O.S bracelets. I'll give you yours when we get home."

Rina tilts her head and the sheriff taps his neck gently, making her blush. Clearly a sign that her bracelet is going to be like her collar. Now I feel a little jealous. Does Daddy not want to collar me?

He walks over and crouches behind me, kissing my neck. "Don't look so sad, baby. I'll collar you when you're ready because I know you're mine, but there are steps. I just told you I'm in love with you," he whispers in my ear.

"Oh," I whisper with a blush, and he chuckles.

"Don't worry, little miss. You are mine in every way there is, and I will collar you. I just want you to be at peace first so you can really enjoy it." He kisses below my ear, making me shiver.

"Okay, Daddy," I tell him with a smile before the guys leave us alone to play again. "Oooo SP, can I has the purple shovel?" I ask Lana, the nickname coming without thought. Trent calls her sweet pea, so it just kind of slipped out.

"Aww I has a nickname now? So. Cool." She hands me the purple shovel and grabs the lime green crab, burrowing it into the sand.

"Yep, yep!" I say, digging a hole into the sand and tossing the waste over my shoulder. I'm digging for gold here. "Pixie Sticks has one too!"

Rina giggles at her new nickname that piggy-backs off what Travis calls her. "I'm totally sweet as sugar. Ohh!" She looks mischievous. "Daddy! Can I has some pixie sticks on the way home?"

"We'll see, baby."

"Well, darn. That didn't go as planned." She huffs and tosses the pale to the side. "Watcha' diggin' for, Abbs?"

"Gold. There has to be gold somewhere, right?" I say, biting my lip. "I is on a mission!"

Lana giggles, lifting the crab up and walking him over to me. "Crabby crab says there's no treasure," she sighs sadly. "He's been all over this land and there is no such fortune to be found."

"Well that's a bummer." I pout before we all fall into a fit of giggles.

"It's totes a bummer. Oohhh, maybe we can talk our daddies into organizing a treasure hunt sometime! That would be so super cool!" Rina says, and we both nod in agreement.

"I heard you three plotting something to do with us so decided we'd better call it a day," Trent's voice booms, and we all groan.

"But Daddy, it was innocent, I swear!"

"Sure it was, sweet pea," he agrees with a smile.

"It was! We were thinking you guys could set up a treasure hunt for us one day," Lana tells him.

"Huh, that is a thought. Maybe we'll plan it when Serenity is more secure and we've gotten some time under our belts," D says, and Lana rolls her eyes.

"So like, next year?" I sass, cutting her off before she sticks her foot in her mouth. Cause the look her Daddy is giving her right now? Hooo boy. I totally just saved her butt.

"If you're lucky and behave like the good girls we know you can be," D says, pulling me up and out of the sandbox before leaning in to whisper in my ear. "You're lucky I noticed that was all to save my sister from getting her ass walloped, little miss, or you'd be in trouble."

"I'm not?" I whisper back, and he shakes with silent laughter.

"Nah, Lana was about to stick her foot in her mouth really bad. I think Trent is even thankful you stopped her from that punishment."

"Oooohhhhh," I say, pulling back to smile at him. "Hi, Daddy."

"Hey, baby. Ready to go have some dinner and watch a movie?" He wiggles his brows, and I giggle.

"Sure, Daddy." Turning, I hug Lana and Rina before saying goodbye and letting D lead me away, knowing I'm about to be fed before I get some very delicious orgasms from the man I love.

## CHAPTER 39
## DAMEON

"Fuck, yes! Holy fuck!" Abigail cums on my tongue for the third time since we moved to the couch. She's so fucking drenched for me, I can't get enough.

"Again," I order, thrusting two fingers into her still spasming cunt as I attack her clit with vigour.

"I can't," she cries, trying to move away from me, but my hold on her one thigh tightens even more.

"You can. One more and then you can have my cock. You want my cock, don't you, sweetness?" I taunt, hardening my tongue and flicking it against her clit repeatedly until she's shaking.

"Yes. Yes, God, yes," she cries, vibrating from the pleasure of my tongue and fingers pushing her to new heights of pleasure. It's as much a declaration of love from me as it is a slight punishment for her sass at dinner.

My little miss decided it would be a good idea to throw a mild tantrum over having to eat broccoli and stuck her tongue out at me, so I warned her if she did it again, I'd make her cum multiple times before she got my cock. Guess she didn't quite see that as a punishment.

"I fucking love when you beg for my cock," I growl against her cunt as she squirms, trying to take me deeper at the same time she tries to run away. Her mind and body can't decide what they truly want, but I know. Despite what she says, she wants to cum again. If it was truly too much to handle, she'd use her safeword.

"Fuck, Daddy, please! Oh!" she screams, and her pussy locks around my fingers as she comes apart once again, riding the pleasure only I can give her.

"Fuck!" I hiss, fighting my fingers free when she starts to let up. Wrapping my arms around her back, I lift her up and sit down, letting her straddle me. "God, you're stunning. Ride my cock, baby."

"Finally!" Abigail holds my cock as she raises up onto her shaky legs, lining me up with her entrance and sinking down. "Yesssssss," she moans.

"God, I love you, baby," I tell her, my hands gripping her ass as she begins bouncing up and down on my cock like she fucking owns it.

"I love you," she moans, leaning forward to kiss me as her arms circle my neck. "I love you, I love you, I love you. Mmmm, I love your cock," she chants with every bounce.

I bark out a laugh, groaning when she joins me, causing her to tighten down on my aching dick. "I love you too, sweetness. I also happen to love the way your sweet pussy worships my cock."

Squeezing her ass, I lift her up a few inches so I can fuck up into her with a primal urge to make her mine and mark her with my release so everyone knows she's fucking mine. Mine.

"Oh, oh, uuuhhhnnnn," Abigail groans and cries, digging her nails into my neck as I fuck her hard and fast.

"That's it, baby. Take my cock like my good girl," I praise her, lowering her down to meet my every thrust, going deeper and deeper until she's a blabbering, incoherent mess. "If it's too much, tap my shoulder twice then pinch, baby. Remember your non-verbal cues."

Abigail kisses me hard, pushing her tongue into my mouth as a way of thanks as she starts fucking down onto me. "Cum for me, Daddy," she whispers into my mouth.

I feel my cock swell at her words and know I can't deny her or myself. I need to mark her now that she knows I love her. "You want me to cum inside of this pussy, sweetness?" I ask her, wrapping my hand up in her hair and tugging.

"Yes, fuck yes, please!" she begs, and I kiss her with all the love and passion I feel for her as she rides me into another orgasm, pulling me along with her.

"Christ, Abigail!" I growl as I cum with her, pulling her tightly into my body as we ride out our orgasms together. "Baby, God, I love you so fucking much." I kiss her reverently, loving the sweet little moan she lets out.

"Mmmm, I love you too, D," she says as she rests her head on my chest. "So fucking much it scares me sometimes."

"Yeah, I get that, baby. But I promise you, I'm not ever going to hurt you or leave. Never." It's a vow I know I can keep because this woman was fucking made for me.

"Were you serious when you said you want to collar me?" she asks quietly, almost like she's afraid I've changed my mind.

"Abigail Davies, are you mine?" I ask.

"Yes, Dameon, I am. All yours," she vows, pulling back to look at me. She's so fucking gorgeous like this, claiming to belong to me, that my greedy dick does a little jump still inside her. "Ooo, someone likes that, huh?" She giggles.

"More than you know, sweetness. And yeah, baby, I mean it." I cup her cheek, running my thumb across her reddened lips. "When you're finally at peace from everything going on so you can make that decision, free and clear? I'll collar you immediately, baby."

"Promise?"

"More than promise, Abigail. It's a fucking guarantee."

"Okay."

"Actually," I say, moving my hands to her hips and grinding her against me. My dick is hard again, thinking about her wearing my collar for anyone in the lifestyle to know she's owned. "We can look at some tomorrow. You can pick your top three, and I will make the final decision."

"Ohhh, o—okay," she moans, our mixed releases helping me slide in and out of her tight core with ease.

It's going to be a long fucking night. Pun very

much intended.

# CHAPTER 40
# ABIGAIL

"Congratulations, Abigail. You're officially graduated!" Mrs. Reedman says when I hand her the final exam.

"We'll see. I don't know if I passed yet," I joke. Hopefully I passed, but I know I've been off my game too, so who knows for certain.

"Abigail, you passed. Even if you were to horribly flunk this exam, your grades are still way above average," she tells me, packing everything away in her bag. "But you didn't fail. You are one of the smartest and most determined people I have ever met, and I know you passed this test just fine."

"Thank you, Mrs. Reedman. For everything," I tell her, feeling myself getting emotional.

"Always, Abigail. It was my pleasure." She comes

over and squeezes my shoulder with a gentle smile. "Close up the room when you're done, alright?"

I nod and thank her with a hug before she leaves, letting me pack up my bag quickly. It's less than a minute after she left that I'm exiting the room, pulling out my phone to let Dameon know I'm on my way him, when someone grabs me from behind, covering my mouth.

"Don't say a fucking word, you little bitch," the man hisses as he starts dragging me away from the classroom.

I scream and fight against him, but he's bigger and stronger than me, so I get absolutely nowhere. Tears start streaming down my face as fear rushes through my very being as I'm being dragged like a puppet through an almost empty school.

"Get in here, you moron, before that idiot finds her!" I hear my father hiss. The reminder of his very existence angers me enough that I start to fight again. In the midst of it all, the cool metal of the bracelet D gave me hits my neck.

I stop fighting and reach over to push the panic button, knowing D will save me. He's just down the hall in the principal's office waiting for me. If my father thought he'd get past Dameon Easton, he's dumber than I took him for.

Not only will D save me, but Sheriff Colt is now on his way as well. I'm safe, and D was right. He's about to become my father's worst fucking nightmare, and I can't wait to witness it.

## DAMEON

I'm so fucking proud of Abigail graduating early. Even after everything her father put her through and her recovery, she was able to push through it all. She's so goddamn strong, and I have every intention of praising her the moment we get home.

My phone buzzes in my pocket, making me smile for a split second before I hear screaming coming down the hall. "Help. Please, help!"

I jump from my seat, catching Hugh's eyes as he does the same.

"What's going on, Mrs. Reedman?" he asks her, and alarm bells go off in my head. She's the teacher that was with Abigail.

Checking my phone, I see the S.O.S signal and curse, dialling Travis. "I got it, I'm on my way there. Don't fucking kill anyone, Dameon. I'm two minutes out."

"No promises," I growl into the phone, hanging up so I can track exactly where she is.

"Billings!" the teacher cries. "He grabbed Abigail right outside of the classroom and took her!"

I don't stay to listen, leaving Hugh to handle the teacher. But I do know one thing. If Travis doesn't get here before I get my hands on that bastard, I'm going to fucking kill him.

Making my way through the halls, I keep my footsteps as silent as I can when I hear arguing coming from around the corner.

"You'll never get away with this," Abigail hisses, and I smirk at the fight in her voice.

Good girl.

"That's where you're wrong, sweet daughter," the mayor's voice slithers out. "I have friends who want those Easton bastards and the Sheriff to fucking burn. I'll make sure you all get what's coming to you."

That's what he thinks, but he's sorely mistaken. Grabbing my phone, I hit the record button, deciding we're going to bring Davies and Boon down once and for all. I will not have the women I love be in danger any longer.

"Sorry to burst your bubble, Mayor," I say, walking around the corner after pocketing my phone. The second I do, Billings starts to look afraid, and he should be. He has his hands on my woman, and I threatened to kill him the last time I was here.

He must loosen his grip just enough from shock because Abby turns on him, punching him hard in the nose until blood spews everywhere.

Billings cries like the little bitch he is as he grips his face.

"Jesus Christ, good help is really hard to find," Davies snarls as he latches onto my girl's arm before kicking Billing's in the head, knocking him out cold.

"Let her go, Davies, or your body is the one they'll find," I warn him, a nicety on my part if you ask me.

"Go fuck yourself, Easton!" he spits out my last name like it's dirt on his expensive leather shoes. "You think I'm going to unhand the little bitch that ruined my entire life?" he snaps, and I roll my eyes like I'm bored with his drama.

"You ruined your entire life, not Abigail." I move my eyes to her. "You good, Abbs?"

"I—I'm fine," she says weakly, and I really want to kill the man.

"Shut up, bitch!" He yanks on her arm, and I see red.

"I said let her go, Davies."

"You know," he starts, "Senator Boon wants this entire town to burn to the ground, your bitch of a sister included." He smiles, and I grind my teeth. "Seems you're all behind his son being killed? Funny thing, that."

"I wasn't aware you were friends with the Senator," I state, carefully goading him on.

"Oh, I wasn't. Not until he saw me as a way to bring all of you down. With promised revenge for me, I was all too happy to oblige, of course." Wow, he really is an idiot. He's also drunk if the smell is anything to go by.

"And just how were you expecting to take us all down?" I question, taking a small step toward them.

"Simple, really. That incompetent idiot sheriff is already in my office. All it will take is orchestrating a meeting there with all of you, and BOOM! Bye bye, assholes."

"You seem to be forgetting one thing," I state, taking another couple of steps. He's so lost in his own taunting game he doesn't seem to notice my closeness.

"And what's that?" he sneers.

"We protect our women with everything we have. And they're never alone."

# CHAPTER 41
## ABIGAIL

I CAN'T BELIEVE THAT ASSHOLE LET MY FATHER IN here. What the fuck did he do, sneak him in through the back door? Jesus. At least he's unconscious on the floor and bleeding. Pity I only got one swing in though.

"Oh, for fuck's sake. They're not precious, delicate flowers that will wither away if you leave them alone," my father snarls at D, but I know what he's doing. My father would too if he wasn't drunk off his ass like the pathetic loser he is.

"That's where you're wrong," Travis, the sheriff Dad and this senator apparently want dead, says, rounding the corner with his gun aimed ahead.

"Oh look, almost the whole gang is here," Dad says with a laugh, causing panic to course through me. Shit. Was this the plan all along? Is he going to blow up the goddamn school or something?

D catches my eye and subtly shakes his head before he taps two of his fingers on his leg to get my attention. The second I see it, I know he wants me to try and break free from my father, but I'm not sure I can with how hard his hold is on me.

When D went over silent cues with me a few days ago after I'd read it in a book, I never thought we'd ever actually use them. We had discussed the possibility of using them when I'm old enough to go to the BDSM club with him in three years, but I mean come on. How the hell was I supposed to know we'd need it now? Funny how life works sometimes, I suppose.

"Dad," I say, trying to pull his attention off of the gun pointed at him.

"Shut up, bitch," he sneers at me, spit flying from his mouth, but his eyes don't leave the gun held on him. "What are you going to do, Sheriff? Shoot me like you did Boon's son?"

"If I have to in order to save Abigail, you better believe I won't hesitate, Davies," Travis says calmly.

It's kind of impressive how unmoving he is holding a weapon that could easily take my father's life. Though, he wouldn't really be a good cop if he couldn't handle stress.

"So you're a cold-blooded murderer then?" Dad asks him, making me roll my eyes. "The townspeople should be so proud."

Catching D's eye again, I give him a nod to hopefully let him know I have a plan. I'm just waiting for the right moment to make my move. When he winks, I know he understands me, and I've never been so fucking thankful for his uncanny ability to read me as I am right now.

"They expect me to protect the citizens of Haven Hills, Davies. Something you'd know nothing about given the abuse you've brought upon your own daughter for almost a decade." Travis is so calm when he says it, but I can see the tick of the nerve in his jaw, proving just how uncalm he really is. It's something Rina told me about once after we became friends and she'd mentioned everything her own father had done.

"This little bitch deserves more for killing my wife, just like you—AH!" Dad screams when I whirl around and bite the hand holding me before punching him in the dick and running into Dameon's arms.

Fuck him for trying to blame me for my mother's

death. It wasn't my fault, and I'm sick and tired of listening to his bullshit.

A shot rings through the air, deafening me as Dad screams again and falls to the ground.

"Shh, baby, it's alright. He's going to live." D cradles me in his arms. I can't understand why he's trying to calm me until I realize I'm screaming from everything and can't seem to stop. "Abigail, I need you to breathe. Right now."

The steel in his voice helps me take a deep, shuddering breath and allowed my piercing scream to die as I take another and another. I hadn't realized I'd stopped breathing. Jesus, I'm a fucking mess.

"S—sorry," I stutter, taking another deep breath. "I didn't..." I shake my head. "I didn't realize I was screaming."

"It's okay, sweetness. It's a lot to take in, but Travis didn't kill the bastard. Pity, really," he mutters, making me snort.

"No shit." I slap my hand over my mouth with wide eyes as I look up at him. I can't believe I just said I wish Travis had killed my father, but D just smirks at me with a glint of amusement in his eye.

"That's my girl," he says, leaning forward and kissing my forehead.

"You fucking prick!" Dad shouts. "I'll have you fired for this!"

"Dad!" I snap, feeling completely safe in Dameon's arms. It's time I tell him what a piece of shit he is. "Shut the fuck up. No one cares, you hear me?" I snarl as D's arms wrap around me.

"You—"

"SHUT. UP! You're finished. The world knows you're a piece of shit human, and we don't want to fucking hear it!" I yell, really feeling heated. "I didn't kill Mom and you fucking know it." He looks stunned as I keep going. "You used it as an excuse to transfer your pain to me when you should have held and loved me like a father is supposed to do. You are garbage. Shut the fuck up and suffer because that gun shot in your leg isn't even a slice of what you've put me through. Stop being a little bitch and take it."

"Holy shit," D cackles behind me, his entire body shaking with laughter as he holds my vibrating body. "Let it all out, sweetness."

"I would if you let me go," I growl, fighting against his hold while shooting daggers at my speechless father.

"As much as I'd love to watch you exact your

vengeance against him, I can't, baby. Travis will have a fit," he says, and the good sheriff groans.

"Abby, I'd love to let you at the bastard but I can't," Travis admits sadly. "This has to be above level, understand?" he asks, and I deflate.

"Fine, but he deserves so much fucking worse than what he's gotten."

"Don't worry, baby. I think he's about to enter a whole new world of hell where he's headed," D says excitedly, and I level my eyes with the sperm donor that helped give me life.

"I hope you suffer where you're going, and I hope it never fucking stops. Get bent, asshole." I break from Dameon and head toward the front of the school, ready to leave this place and never return.

When I walk out of those doors, I'm leaving my demons behind me for good.

## EPILOGUE

ABIGAIL

"Abby, can you come here please?" D calls from his office, and I swallow the nerves down.

It's been two weeks since the showdown with my father at the school, and it's been a freaking whirlwind. Dad was placed in maximum security prison for another attempt on my life, not that he got that far because D was incredible. The evidence he gathered recording the shit with my father was enough to put him away for good. Not to mention the senator's arrest and upcoming trial.

Dad pled guilty before the judge once he knew the recording existed, forgoing the embarrassment of a trial, and I'm glad because I just want to be finished with that chapter of my life.

"Coming!" I shout back, taking a deep breath as I

head to the man I love, knowing it's time for my punishment. We'd talked about it last night, and I told him I was ready to receive whatever he felt was appropriate for my trying to steal Star and run away, and I am.

We waited a few weeks because for several days after the encounter, I woke up with nightmares and struggled so hard with wanting to cut again, even relapsing once. But I don't want to wait anymore. I want to clear this guilt I've felt for my behaviour so we can move forward.

"Hey, baby," he greets me when I walk through the door.

He's sitting at his desk with one of the butt plugs he'd ordered for me sitting on a cloth beside a bottle of lube. Oh, yay, butt stuff.

"Hi, Daddy," I say sheepishly. "So, butt stuff, huh?"

"Partly. You okay with that?" he checks in with me, and I nod.

"Uh-huh," I tell him truthfully. "I mean, yes, Daddy. Just nervous."

"Good girl for using your actual words before I had to correct you," he praises me, pulling me over to the desk. "Strip for me, baby."

I blink at him momentarily before doing as he

says, removing my sweats and tank top until I'm standing before him naked. I love how desirable he makes me feel as his hungry eyes rake over my body.

"God, you're a vision, baby," he whispers. "I'm so fucking in love with you."

I blush, feeling warm all over. "I love you too, Daddy. So much."

"Come here, baby." D holds his hand out and I take it, moving closer to him. "I want to tell you what's going to happen, alright?"

I nod and smile. "Yeah, I think that works best. Thanks, Daddy."

"Always, sweetness. I will never give you a punishment without first knowing what you're getting into, alright?"

"Yes, Daddy."

"Good. Okay, first, I'm going to plug you and have you stand in the corner for five minutes." I fidget, feeling nervous, but he squeezes my hand reassuringly. "Normally, you'd have to stay silent, but I don't like that idea for you with how your brain likes to spiral, so we're going to have a little discussion with your nose in the corner, yes?"

"Yes, Daddy."

"Good girl. We'll start with that and see how

you're feeling afterward okay? Or do you want to know what else I have planned?"

"All, please, Daddy," I tell him, squeezing his hand harder to ground me.

"Okay, baby. After that, I'm going to have you sit on my cock and write the line *'I will not run from Daddy and put my life in danger.'* fifty times."

I gasp. "Fifty?! While you're fucking me?" I squeak.

"No, you're just going to sit on my cock to remind you that I own you." He looks devilish. "I told you I didn't need impact play to be a sadist, sweetness. Watching you squirm on my dick will be euphoric for me."

"God, that's so mean," I whimper, making him chuckle darkly.

"No, mean would be not letting you cum after, which I almost wasn't going to," he says. "But then I remembered how proud of you I am for breaking that prick Billing's nose and for standing up to your father, and decided you deserved to cum at the end of this."

"Oh thank fuck!" I sign in relief.

"On the guarantee you will never try to run away again, especially on an animal you don't even know how to ride." He looks at me sternly, and I nod like a bobble head.

"I promise. No more running."

"Good girl. Come and bend over the desk and stick that gorgeous ass out for me," he orders, and I do as I'm told, feeling exposed as he moves in behind me.

He grabs the plug and lube, clicking the top open behind me. "Spread your cheeks, baby," he says, and I groan but do as he says. This punishment is already gonna suck. I'm not going to make it worse by losing the chance to cum.

I feel his wet fingers run along my crack, spreading the lube. "Take a deep breath in. Good girl, now let it out," he guides as he slowly slides the plug into place.

It's such a weird feeling. It doesn't exactly hurt, but it's stretching me more than I've felt before.

"That's my girl," D praises, helping me to stand. "Now go stand over there. Nose in the corner with your ass out, and we're going to have a chat." He walks over to the corner with me, helping me into position.

"Don't leave," I beg, and his hand rests on my lower back.

"I wasn't planning on it, baby, but I'll keep my

hand right here, okay?" When I nod, he continues. "Normally, I think this conversation would happen over my lap, but since spanking isn't an option, I think this will work well."

"Okay, Daddy." I close my eyes and take a deep breath.

"Why are you being punished right now?"

"Because I tried to run away?" I ask quietly, not sure of my answer.

"In a sense, but it's more than that. You put yourself in danger. If Star had let you take her out, you could have been seriously hurt or even killed. Do you know how scary that is for me to think about?"

Well, when he puts it like that.

"But I wasn't trying to get hurt, I was scared," I tell him, feeling the tears build.

"I know you were, baby, but I need you to trust me and come to me with your fears from now on okay?"

"Yes, Daddy." I sniff, the first tear starting to fall.

"Good girl. You also could have hurt Star if she'd allowed you to take her out."

"Oh no!" I cry, the damn breaking as I think about that.

I never wanted to hurt Star, and honestly, I hadn't even thought about that being a possibility.

"Shhh baby, it's alright. All is forgiven when this is done, I just want you to see how scary it was from every angle, okay?" D consoles me, rubbing my back as I cry my heart out.

"O-okay," I cry. "I'm s—sorry."

"Shh, I know you are, baby. Come here, sweetness." He stands me up and pulls me into his arms, comforting me the way only he knows how.

"Daddy," I cry, my whole body feeling weak as I continue to sobbing.

"Hey, hey, it's okay." He holds me tighter. "I think that's your limit for punishment right now, huh?" he says, surprising me. "As your Dom and Daddy, it's up to me to see when you can't handle anymore, even if you don't use your safeword."

"God, I love you," I cry into him, holding him as tight as I can. "Please don't ever leave me."

"Oh, baby, that's never going to happen." He pulls me over to the desk to sit me down on his lap. "Open the top drawer, sweetness."

I look at him in confusion with tears still running down my cheeks, unable to stop them. Pulling the drawer open, I see a velvet box and cry harder as I take it out.

"Open it," D says, and I do, gasping in shock when one of my collar choices is inside. "Abigail

Davies, will you be my submissive, my little, and the love of my life for the rest of our lives?" D asks, and I nod, staring down at the beautiful rainbow slave collar.

I'm not D's slave, but it's just so beautiful and perfect, it felt right to want that one. I wasn't sure he'd choose it, but he must have agreed it was the right one for us since it's the one he chose.

"Yes!" I throw my arms around him. "Yes, yes, yes, yes, yes! A thousand times yes!"

He chuckles and grabs my neck, kissing me deeply. "Good, because you belong to me, Abigail. And I belong to you." He kisses me again and pulls another, smaller box from the drawer.

"What's that?"

"Oh, this? It's a matching bracelet for me to wear, sweetness. You own me just as much I own you, understand?"

"I—I get to collar you too?"

He smiles, kissing me gently.

"Yeah, baby you do."

**THE END**

## AFTERWORD

Whew! This book was another emotional ride for me, but I loved every second of it.

Travis and Rina have been in my head for months, yelling at me and demanding their story to be told and they were none too happy about being made to wait haha.

When the idea for the Serenity Stables series came to me, I knew I wanted it to be different than my other books. I wanted each book to address something real that many people struggle with and so far I've chosen things I personally connect with.

There's always a story behind someone's smile, and mine hasn't always been the happiest.

What Rina goes through as an individual with BPD is some of my own personal experiences with it, but is in no means how it affects everyone.

Like I said in the preface, if you've met one person with BPD you've met one person. We're all different and unique with our own stories to tell.

Thank you so much for taking the time to read these stories and I hope they help bring you some joy. <3

# ALSO BY CASSIE HARGROVE

## Suited Up Daddies

1: Daddy's Naughty Secretary

2: Daddy's little Novice

3: Daddy's Proper Present

4: Daddy's Precious Rose

5: Daddy's Sexy Sub

6: Daddy's Perfect Pair

Box Set with Bonus Novella

## Serenity Stables

1: Healing with Daddy

2: A Home with Daddy

3: Rescued by Daddy (Coming Soon)

## Connerton Academy

(A College Paranormal Why Choose Romance)

1: Freshman Firsts

2: Sophomore Secrets

3: Junior Justice

4: Senior Sacrifices

## **The Revenge Diaries**

(A Series of Dark/Very Dark Standalones)

1: Trick or Revenge

2: Beautiful Revenge (Original and Less Triggering Versions)

3: Love's Dark Revenge (Coming Soon)

## **Standalones**

Depravity: An Extremely Taboo Novel (Co-Write with Seven Rue)

The Art of Freedom and Growth (A Depravity Extended Epilogue) (Co-Write with Seven Rue)

## **The Deadly Seven**

A Co-Write with Story Brooks

1: Obsession

2: Seduction

3: Devotion

4: Salvation

5: Justified Retribution: Kristen's Story (Coming March 2023)

Deadly Seven Boxsets Vol. 1&2 with Bonus Content

## Dark Series

1: Dark Torment

2: Dark Longing

3: Dark Adoration (Coming Later in 2023)

## Erotic Shorts

Taken By Him

Intern-al Affairs

Bound To Him

Santa Daddy's Naughty Baby

CASSIE HARGROVE WRITING AS A.L. RYAN

## Standalones

Roommates: A Dark Sapphic Romance

## Forbidden Kinks

Book 0.5:

Still His

Previously Published as Still by Cassie Hargrove

# ACKNOWLEDGMENTS

First and foremost, I want to thank the readers who have given me a chance and fallen in love with the characters in my head.

I love writing about Daddies and their littles and I have no intentions of stopping :).

Always, thank you to my husband for being supportive and understanding as I lose sleep because my brain won't shut off and more characters and ideas come to play!

My best friend and cover designer, Jade I fucking love you every single day! None of this would be possible without your belief and support.

My beta team of readers, you guys are the bomb dot com and I love your input! Thank you!

# ABOUT THE AUTHOR

Cassie Hargrove is an emerging author of all things romance. She is a stay at home mom to 3 children. Twins age 8 (both have severe autism) and a sassy and rambunctious 5 year old.

She is a photographer in her spare time and lives with her husband, kids, dog, and 3 cats. She has been writing most of her life and recently chose to share that love and passion with the world.

Writing brings an element of calm in the chaos that is life.